Wail of the Wyrm

or

Report: Jaspur Mud Wastes*

The first name is my idea of what this book should be called. Arvi doesn't think it needs anything more than what he handed in to Meagan. We couldn't agree, so you get both of them. -Turner

Listen to a playlist curated for this book!

ISBN: 978-1-955639-15-6

To Mom:
Thanks for being the best friend a gal could ever ask for.

Table of Contents

Introduction

Mud. It's really only wet dirt, isn't it? And dirt is what started the fascinating correspondence between Earth and that far off planet of Planistah. I don't know where the planet is. I don't know the whole story of how people got there. But I do know people are there. Real people, human beings, *homo sapiens*, and all that. You can go and find my first introduction to the *Dreaded King Saga* if you wish to hear more on that topic. Though I suppose, really, you will have to read right through to the end of the *Saga* to learn everything I know of it.

But right now I'm more concerned about the second dirt. Not mud, not at the moment, that comes later. I mean the second time Turner Hitchley and his pals used the Planistah method of lightning and dirt to send a box of interesting items and documents to a field wherein I was living in a barn waiting for said box. One of the documents is what you are now holding.

In fact they sent a whole boxed set, very nicely leather bound. It looks quite keen on Vera and I's mantle.

Oh, before I forget, there's one more thing you need to know (if somehow you missed the five-book saga translated so expertly by my humble self). Planistah is, as has been mentioned, a different planet. Which means time there is not the same as here. Well, time itself is, if you can define time (don't try, you'll get a headache). But how they count it is not the same. It is a smaller planet than our Earth, and their sun rises and sets twice in one of their days. The people there divide their time into five-hour increments; a sunny morning, a dark afternoon, a sunny night, and a dark night. This, if you are doing the math correctly, equals out to twenty-hour days. Now, back to the more interesting bits than math (blech!).

It seems that Arvi and Turner took to adventuring. Well, I suppose a better way to put it is that Arvi took Turner on his adventuring. As a knight, *the knight*, really, the best there is on Planistah, Arvimeer Aytenmar is called away quite often to fix things. You see, when a sheriff or the lawkeeper are having difficulties eradicating a do-badder, or become baffled by the mystery of some unknown causing problems, they send for help from higher up. The highest high up are the Cleangal Knights, the personal bodyguards for the king himself. Meagan, the Chief Knight, is their leader. And Arvimeer Aytenmar, Heir of the Cleangal House of Shards, Protector of the King, Chief

Courtier, Wielder of Peace, is the best of the knights Meagan has at his command.

So, when something comes up that others are having trouble dealing with, Arvi is at the top of the line for "seeing to it." He is sent off on difficult missions more often than he is allowed to protect the king at the castle. And there is nothing mundane about his work, I must say!

At one point, he and Turner got tired of trying to explain their adventures to the many people who kept asking. So they began to write them down. A shrewd businessman, Hembleton Iggreesson, got wind of it. He immediately bombarded their door and practically begged on his knees for the right to manage their publishing. Arvi, shrewd businessman himself, only sort of let him manage it. But between Iggreesson and the obvious interest of the stories themselves, Arvi and Turner's *Knight Jobs* have become a sensation upon Planistah. They were kind enough to send us a complete set of the volumes they currently have published.

What you hold in your hands is the first. I hope you enjoy it as much as I enjoyed translating a new tale from the world of Charlom Hartsom, Dreaded King of Planistah.

-Arthur A. Simpson

The piercing growl pulsated around him. It rang and vibrated in his bones as the man stumbled through the mud. Only darkness filled his vision. Even his feet were hidden by the dark as he sloughed and slipped at a frenzied run. His own frantic breaths were drowned out by the scream of the beast, as if his life was already gone to this thing. Hou Merguson whimpered, nearly sobbing, as he slipped and pounded through the stinking Jaspur mud. He didn't notice anything but the terror turning him into a slobbering, begging coward as he ran. The nightmarish sound of the beast's screams went on. All around him, it was everywhere. The unearthly noise rang through the dark. It pierced through him, shaking his quivering heart with its volume.

He was going to die. Merguson knew it. That was the worst part, he knew he was going to die, and there was nothing he could do about it. No help, no one to turn to out here in the dark in the stinking muddy hills, nowhere to run. He had run. He had run for what felt like a lifetime, till his breath spewed out of him in a hissing rattle and he couldn't suck in enough oxygen.

That call, the eerie up and down shriek. The roar. The growl. The triumphant hunting call of the leermackle. It was said anyone who heard it was dead already. No one escaped a hunting leermackle. And the beast had its sights set on him. Merguson slipped on the mud again, sprawled on the hill, and rolled helplessly through the sludge. Incomprehensible pleas and prayers poured from him through his desperate, hissing breaths, but he was too far gone to care.

Something whipped over his head. He felt the icy air of it as he struggled to his feet. A hoarse cry ripped from him and he stumbled back, slipping again on the mud. Again that hiss of air came, something large and sharp whistling through the darkness.

This time it didn't miss.

Chapter 1: The First Severed Heads! or Beginning *

T he beast has ravaged for the last time."

"Are you sure ravaged is the right word?"

"Wrecked? Despoiled? Wantonly destroyed? Choose what terms thou wilt, the meaning is the same."

"It ain't all destroyed! Besides, last time, you said *then* it was the last time."

"Reminding me of my indecision is not helping thy case. Or hers," I commented dryly. Turner's mouth clamped shut and we stared at his dragon. Quinty sat in our kitchen, in the midst of the disarray she had caused, hiding her head behind her wings in shame. Half eaten boxes and their contents, fruit pits and peelings, the bones from the leftover vol, the wreckage surrounded the little beast. Flour splayed all about the kitchen. It stuck to the floor from the sticky remains of the fruit, and traveled nearly to the ceiling on the left-hand side.

"One thing is certain," I said, "I am not helping thee clean the mess."

*Truth, we still can't agree. I think you're going get two names throughout this book. -Turner

"Aw, Arvi!"

"I wouldst not even if I had the time, for thou must learn to either train thy creature or take the consequences."

"It ain't often she's done this in the three years she's been here," Turner grumped, and I stared upon him. "All right, so only about once a couple of months, that ain't that much."

"'Is not' is the proper term. I have not the time to argue with thee, I am called to the chief knight's rooms."

"Truth?" I couldst almost see curiosity pricking his ears and brightening his eyes. "I wonder where yourn being sent off to this time?"

"'You are,' Turner, thou knows the correct methods of address now and ought to use them," I commented as I swiftly strapped Peace back on my belt (and ignored the way his eyes rolled at me). "I know not why I am required. Do not forget thy studies, and the kitchen had best be clean upon my return!" I added over my shoulder as I strode from the door.

I was glad I could not hear the boy muttering as I trotted from the trees into the castle and toward the chief knight's quarters. Turner had grown in many ways, I reminded myself. But I sometimes thought his impudence too had

grown, especially these past months. This year, since the lad had turned thirteen, his sauciness had taken a turn for the worse (a thing which I never guessed couldst happen, for I had thought it as high a level as it couldst attain). It was not that I required much of the boy. He even had time twice a week to spend away from his studies and in the Trosk workshop. I was near certain he took more time from his studies than I had strictly granted, to spend with Layah and Tilmey, and studied at nights in his room to compensate. But we have an unspoken agreement; he does not ask for leave and I do not inquire. Yet still he complained of the heaviness of his load, and ever wished me to lessen his studies. I did not lessen *my* duties, many a lonely road had I trod when rather I wouldst be elsewhere.

But it was not the time for me to ponder it now. Servant Meagan awaited me.

I found the great man leaning over his desk in his rooms, papers piled high about him and a scowl upon his face. He did not lift his eyes to me as I entered his quarters and bowed. It took him near a half minute to acknowledge me enough to say I couldst rise. His manner did not surprise me, it had been so ever since Harry Arnbolt begun his regime of demanding written

records from Charlie's staff. Servant Meagan did not appreciate the joys of paperwork.

"Arvi," he growled as I straightened before him, "what do you know about leermackles?"

"A very large beast, nearly as long as three hay carts according to some accounts. They are built like a great wyrm, with plates of hard bone jutting up along the back. Their method of locomotion is to shift their thick body from side to side over the ground, as a snake using the action of a sidewinder. The leermackle has been known to reach speeds of ninety miles per hour, though it can keep to such bursts of speed for only a short period of time. It can travel as fast as the fastest of merthyls for a full day, however, and reportedly show no signs of flagging. Its hunting method is to first decapitate its victim with its razor-edged tail, then slowly engorge it whole, leaving the head where it fell. Unless particularly hungry, in which case it has been known to swallow its victims still alive. It has been speculated, such live victims might continue to live within the beast for some three days, slowly being digested by the leermackle. The leermackle prefers to hunt in the dark, as they are blind and find their food through a spectacular sense of smell, and their incredibly sensitive feelers. Their call is peculiar to

themselves, reaching the uttermost edge of the higher and lower scale of man's hearing. Through a trick of the beast's the unsettling call surrounds a victim, 'wrapping around a soul as a life-sapping blanket of terror,' one author wrote. The last living leermackle reported—"

"Was two days ago," Servant Meagan interrupted and tossed a letter toward me. I clamped my mouth shut as it was in danger of falling open. The paper wast of cheap make with an unpleasing smell, I noted as I lifted it. The missive came from the Jaspur region. A town reported livestock missing, and people disappearing in frightening circumstances. The heads of three people had been found. A frightful animal's call had been heard in the dark times. "Indescribably scary," the author of this letter described it. I looked up at the knight.

"A live leermackle has not been reported for nigh on two hundred years."

"Until now," Servant Meagan rumbled. "Are you willing to take on the assignment? I am aware of the hunting odds for a leermackle. Twelve to three, in the leermackle's favor. I would rather not have you eaten."

"I have no fear of the beast," I murmured, still staring at the letter. A live leermackle? It could not be. Nay, it could not! This was a nightmarish thing which had passed into legend, it had been hunted out of existence as too dangerous and destructive to allow to live in a world with humans. Nothing could live within a thirty mile radius of a hunting leermackle, and it wouldst take but a year to reduce their territory to a lifeless desolation.

"Good. Go this afternoon, and I will expect you back in time for Charlie's Midtime feast," the chief knight said. I waited but a moment more, for his usual benediction. His gaze lifted from the papers in front of him and finally focused upon me. "Go with God, don't die, and don't do too much. Only what is necessary."

I nodded, bowed my leave, and slid out, successfully hiding my amusement. Ever since the paperwork regime, those had been his orders. The less we did, the less he had to write out for Harry Arnbolt.

The morning sun was disappearing on the horizon as I emerged from the castle interior. I heard a bird singing in a lightmot tree and allowed myself a smile at the delightful sound. For an instant I considered traveling straight back to Turner's and my little house. We chose a place situated just without the walls (to allow anyone access to us, both castle inhabitants and those of the townspeople who felt the need).

Then I bethought me the boy wouldst still be striving to clean the dragon's wreckage and be in a foul mood. If I waited but a few minutes more, Turner wouldst slip out to visit his friends. Then I couldst make my exit without his prying eyes and pouting manner.

I wouldst not even speak to him of a leermackle hunt. If this was an actual leermackle, the danger of the quest would be greater than any I had yet encountered. It was no small thing to face such a beast and I would not have the boy fretting. Besides, Turner was behind three chapters in his mathematics. He needed no distractions.

I turned my steps toward Corinth and Charlie's abode. I wouldst see the high prince ere I left for the other side of the world, and bid him be good. It had been some time since I had the leisure to greet the little man. As I strode through the left archway I caught sight of the high prince. He was toddling about the garden in front of the royal apartment, selecting flowers for a bouquet. He plucked just the heads, such that it would be impossible to use them. His mother did not seem to mind. Corinth sat upon the garden bench, Maxil upon one knee and Maysee upon the other. All thought the prince and princess were twins when they met the royal babes. Most were incredulous to hear the lovely Maysee was a Hartsom foundling taken into the royal family. I had a suspicion more would follow soon to swell Charlie and Corinth's budding family tree.

Aston spied me first. He waved his fistful of flowers, gave a prodigious yell, and ran for me, his pudgy legs pounding into the ground. My heart swelled at his greeting, delighted he still looked upon me with such favor. His arms lifted and I scooped him up and spun him upside down as he giggled. As I righted him, the prince began to pour forth his excited babble and laughter. I heard something about mouths, eats, and possibly bowl. Then he gave a great laugh and smashed his fist of flowers onto the top of my head, grinding it in.

"He was going to make a salad, but it seems you became the bowl," Corinth interpreted the babbles, as Aston laughed uproariously. I looked up, an idiotic grin on my face at the high prince's merriment, and found the queen smiling upon me. "How are you, Arvi? It has been ages since you have come visiting the children and me."

"Better than I deserve to be." I sat Aston upon the ground and offered my cloak pocket to help him gather his flowers for his salad. "It was

not my wish to stay away from thee and thine. I have been kept busy these past months."

"So I gathered from Turner," Corinth said, and something in the manner of it bid me look away from the toddling prince to her. "Are you staying in town now?"

"Well..."

"If not, I know he would like to go along with you."

"Well..."

"You just came in again yesterday. From a full month's absence. How did you find your red-haired charge?"

"Cheeky."

"I'm sure," Corinth smiled...though there was something behind the look.

"Is there aught I should know?" I asked, almost reluctantly. I must off to hunt a leermackle, I did not have time for such an interruption. Even as the thought came to me I realized my error, and felt the guilt of it. I had taken the faithful Turner on willingly, even gratefully. He couldst never be "an interruption." When I looked up again I couldst see Corinth knew my thoughts. The guilt only grew greater. She smiled again, mostly at her son as he toddled up to her, accepting a handful of the fruits of Aston's decapitations before the high prince turned him to a mud puddle.

"Did you know Turner was escorted back to your house by the guardsmen, twice this month?"

"What!"

"The second time I asked him why and he scowled and wouldn't give a straight answer. He might answer you though. If you are ever around long enough that he still considers you in charge and deserving of an answer."

"I am not sure I understand thy meaning. He knows our agreement."

"Just think on it. Now, if you could dunk Aston in the water trough for me to clear off some of that mud, I need to start getting these three ready for the presentation of the newest orphanage. Harry thinks it would be a nice gesture to have the whole family at the opening." I duly dunked, carried the high prince to his chambers for the queen, and left to ready my things.

Turner was not at home when I arrived. The kitchen was adequately clean. I put the questions from my mind and turned me to gathering things for my quest.

Two days later, I rode into the town of

Peyson, Jaspur. In truth, it is more of a hamlet. The obligatory pine planks make up the town of some fifty square buildings. Most are two storied affairs, though some reach as high as three, and some to only one story. There is one square building in town which boasts four stories. The sign, squeaking in the wind as it hung over the door, declared it to be the Resin Inn. I drew Kleof to a stop in front of the building and alighted upon the plank walkway. The ordinary ruckus of an inn couldst be heard spewing from the doors. It seemed the leermackle had not scared away the drinking customers. I pushed open the rough door and stepped into the dim interior, sliding naturally to the side to keep from being framed in the sunlight. Silence fell. All eyes in the large room turned to me. There were not many considering the size of the room. Only three old men, two women huddled over a pot of tea, a barmaid, a lanky serving lad, and a burly man I presumed was the innkeeper. That individual was the first to speak.

"You are ah knight," he growled. I gave a little bow. "What is ah knight doing 'ere?"

"He 'as coome about tha beast," one of the women said, hushed awe in her tone. It was very strange to hear Charlie's accent coming from strangers. I merely nodded and stepped farther into the room.

"You are late, as usual," the innkeeper smiled. Not pleasantly. "Tha beast 'as been gone for ovah ah week. It 'as left for whatevah spot it crawled froom in tha first place."

"He is ah sour old crow," one of the women said, "but 'e is telling you tha truth. Tha leermackle is gone."

"I 'eard it, you know," a gray-haired man spoke up from the bar.

"We know, Clairm, you 'ave told us near ah 'undred times by now," one of his companions grumped.

"Tha most frightful thing you could evah 'ear," this Clairm continued, pretending not to hear the interruption. "It was far ooff, which I was glad oof, but it was clear. High and low, it screamed and 'owled! Nevah 'eard anything like it in all my days. I don't mind saying, I went and 'id in my bedroom, with tha door locked."

"That would be tha day Merguson was killed," another took up, with the grisly relish of the old man who has nothing to do but talk. "Nothing left oof 'im but 'is 'ead. A petrified look on 'is muddy face too. Like 'e was struck dead with terror."

"It isn't terror what kills a man when you

only find 'is 'ead," the innkeeper snorted, and looked at me. "What can I do for you?" It seemed more of a threat than an inquiry. But I answered it simply enough.

"I wouldst see where the beast struck last. Can any of thee tell me where that might be?"

"Well, aren't you tha lord, with your thees and thous," the innkeeper sneered.

"Shut up, Mulk. He is ah man who doesn't wait, I like that," Clairm commented, slamming his cup down upon the bar.

"Shush, you old souse. I know where it struck last bettah than any," one of the ladies spoke up. She stood, shifted her shawl over her hair, and began to stride toward the door, beckoning me to follow. I couldst not help noticing she was near a head and a half taller than me. Everyone in this region was tall of stature and large of bone structure; I felt decidedly miniscule. We stepped into the morning light and she began to lead the way at a swift swinging gate. I fell into step just behind her, Kleof following dutifully.

The town of Peyson might be small, but it seemed to be one of the wealthier in Jaspur. The streets were cobbled. The distinctive red mud of the region was still here (tracked in by countless feet and paws), but the stones set neatly together kept out most of it. Yet it was not long before we had stepped past the last building of Peyson. The stones underfoot ceased, and the red mud took over. It was of an odd sort, for it both clung to anything it touched, and caused the foot to slip dangerously. The smell of it struck my nostrils with a savage ferocity. It was not as foul as the dark ways perhaps, but there was a decidedly similar stench. As of years of filth collected and stored, rotting just enough to give off the maximum amount of smell, but never quite enough to leave.

The woman marched on. The buildings of Peyson dropped farther behind until they couldst no longer be seen. Hills began to rise around us. Bare, for the most part, simply round masses of mud. I watched small avalanches of the red mixture forming the hills' shapes as I walked. Some had grass clinging stubbornly to their sides. Most were bare of even that ornament. The woman marched on, past hill after hill. There were no houses out here, and I saw little sign of livestock either. It occurred to me the leermackle had not much work ahead of him to create a waste of this place he had claimed as his territory. The woman suddenly turned from the road. I saw a small herd of vols, ruminating on a patch of grass. The

animals were skinny, small for vols, their coats lackluster and patchy. A sorry looking lot.

But not as sorry as the remains of one of their number. The head rested upon the ground on the far side of the herd, away from the road. It stank, beginning to decompose. But I couldst still see the wound which had severed it. Clean, quick, and precise. Through sinew and bone the blow struck. The vol had likely been unaware of its own death.

"This is my 'usband's 'erd," the woman spoke up. "He wanted ta bury it, ta get it out oof sight. But I said you would want ta see it first."

"I thank thee for thine intervention," I nodded. My gaze cast about the ground. There were tracks here, signs of the beast's fright and his fall, and of something...large. "How long ago was it found?"

"Eight days. You are fortunate it 'asn't rained since then, longest stretch without water I 'ave evah seen in tha rainy season. No tracking on our land, mind. There is no saying what mischief you and your great merthyl might do. Tha beast is gone, we told you. Maybe it choked on a bone, or just went back where it came from. It is no longah 'ere, that we know. I will leave you looking and get back ta my tea." The woman turned on her heel and began to stride for town again. I called a thank you out of courtesy, though I knew those in this region hardly expected such gestures.

There were tracks here...but... They were large and oval, as if a great body had rolled about in the mud, coming from the southwest. That much was correct, and right for a leermackle. But... I had studied leermackle tracks, as faithfully recorded in several volumes. They were always rippled, as the beast flexed its brown sides while it rolled about, and the manner of its travel was uneven, jerking forward in small slides one moment then leaping near eight feet forward the next. They were tapered too, as a leermackle was bulbous at the front and slimmed toward the tail. These tracks beside the vol were large and oval, yes. But they were perfectly even. Simply oval indentions in the ground, gently overlapping each other in a perfect manner.

Whatever had done this deed was not a leermackle.

Chapter 2: Burning Pigs! or Feasting Interlude

The Midtime feast rolled around tonight. I guessed I had better show up at Charlie's celebrations. If I didn't Mrs. Hartsom would be wondering what happened to me and probably send some knight to ask. Besides, I considered as I dug out my fancy stuff, there would be good eats there. But it wouldn't be like the Midtime feasts down in the dark ways. Sure, there weren't that much food maybe, and we was all worked hard and wondering if we would even be alive by the end of the week. But we knew how to put on a festival! Maybe it were because everything was so uncertain, how we all wondered if we'd survive, you know, but when there was a party we all partied. Midtime, there was the tree to burn, and the hogs to throw, and always a host of gigglies to chaw on and laugh over. Everybody'd be laughing. And old Grammy woulda' been right in the midst of things, throwing more hogs than them all and screaming at the tree while it burned. Some days I still missed her...missed her awful.

"Thine hat is smashed," Arvi says behind me. A smile slid over me. Though my head couldn't decide whether it should be a smile, sniffle, or an angry yell. I kept my features even as I turned around. Arvi, splattered with red clay, was stepping into his room just across the hall from mine. He tossed his klackmen on the bed and headed for his wardrobe.

"That's a lot of mud," I called to him.

"Dost thou ever lock the door when I am gone?" he called back as he hunted for his outfit for feasting.

"Sometimes," I answer. The reason I don't lock it now was because I had just come in, and knew I was about to go out again. But I may as well keep that quiet. Arvi shows back up in his fancy stuff. He was already strapping Peace on under his spare cloak, the blue one with the long fancy hood.

"Hurry, or we shall be late to take our seats. That means change thy hat, Turner," he orders as he heads for the door. I sigh and change the hat for one with a green feather that ain't quite as mushed. Then I run to catch up to him, and we trot toward the dining hall. We don't say nothing. But it's kind of nice to have him there anyway. He ain't been around much these past months. Arvi pushes the big old doors open.

A wash of heat hits me, and sudden there's a great sizzling sound and Aston laughing and

Charlie calling things and Corinth calling back, and a host of footsteps running around on the stone ground. I step in quick beside Arvi.

A whole tree is burning in a specially built fireplace in the middle of the hall. A whole tree, its trunk near as wide as my shoulders! It crackles and sizzles and smells of tar already. Charlie's there with Aston and Maysee in his arms. He has little black tar hogs in his hands as he dances around the tree and shows his shorters how to fling them into the fire so's they sizzle and pop. I sudden find a tray full of gigglies stuck in front of my face and Mrs. Hartsom's there, shoving the thing in my arms. She points across the room to the barons and their wives and all, them what are called courtiers for some reason. They's all standing there staring at Charlie and Mrs. Hartsom like they don't know what to do. I laugh and trot toward them, yelling out the calls as I go. We'll teach these stuffy old folks how to really celebrate Midtime!

My tray's soon empty and I turn around to get another, chuckling. I wonder how many of them's going to try and eat the whole thing. My eye catches Arvi and I gotta grin. He's still looking all serious, but he's tossing hogs with Charlie, and showing Miss Dlacey how to do it as her da looks on real confused. I guess my dragging him down into town for a few celebrations has helped. Miss Dlacey catches on fast, and soon she's having a good old time, and teaching other folks how to do it, and she and Mrs. Hartsom are laughing at Aston as he tries his best to eat the gigglies. You can only get 'em to try and eat it once. But it sure is fun to watch that once. Arvi nearly got it down the first time I takes him to a real Midtime feast. Which reminds me to look for my pal as he seems to have slipped away from the fire.

It takes a few minutes for me to spot him. Arvi's hunched in a chair in a corner staring at his feet and scowling. He looks real black. Huh. I head over to ask what's got him so down. But a page gets there first, and steps right up to my pal. The page is holding a yarping out to Arvi and saying something, as he points back over his shoulder at Charlie. Another smile goes over me as I watch Arv take the yarping and slowly get to his feet. Of course, he's the Stroller tonight. Down in the town it's whoever gets picked for it that night, but up here it's more stuffy, and the chief courtier is the Stroller. That phrase, chief courtier, really confused me at first. But it just means the king's favorite, along with the one what has the oldest lineage, and

who can do things best. Obviously that's Arvi. Polite clapping goes around the place as he's noticed, because the Stroller is one even the stuffy nobles is used to at the Midtime Feast. Arvi's hand strokes the strings, getting ready. But I can tell by the look on his face that his mind's only sort of on it. Most of him is still thinking about whatever had him scowling. A chord rings around the place, and Arv's voice follows it in the traditional song.

Except his voice is in a completely different key than the chord. Everyone kind of winces and the smiles get sudden frozen into polite ones. Arvi blinks, and his shoulders square like he's coming out of his thoughts back to us. He fixes his note real quick and launches into the songs for real, and his perfect voice makes everybody forget the rough beginning. In about a minute he has them all dancing around the place, singing along with him like they's supposed to. He's the best musician I's ever heard, of course. Though I like his own songs he plays in our house better than the stuffy ones he plays in public. He don't mess up again. But I don't forget that first mistake. It ain't like him to make a mistake. Ever.

"Turnah! What do you think oof my feasting?" Charlie sudden says beside me. I turn

around to him and grin.

"Not bad, Charlie, not bad at all. The gigglies could be chewier," I answer.

"I will 'ave ta tell tha cook your complaint," he laughs. "You should 'ave seen me trying ta explain what we wanted, 'e thought I was ah madman, you could see it in 'is eyes." Aston gives a shout and throws himself out of his da's arms toward me, and I laugh as I catch him and swing him in a circle.

"What do you think of the hogs, Aston?" I ask him. He holds one up. He must have been holding it for quite a while because his sweaty hand has started to make it leak black all over him. Aston lifts it high and I get ready to help him fling it into the fire. Then it goes to his mouth and he tries to take a big bite of it, as his da and I yell at him not to, trying to get it away from him and not laugh so hard we encourage him. Miss Dlacey is already laughing hard enough she's nearly doubled over.

It were a good Midtime. Charlie concedes some boring parts to the stuffy nobles, and they seem to kind of enjoy the parts he brings in from the streets, and it were real nice. The food was awful good. Arvi and me are near waddling as we come out of the hall into the brightness of the night sun and start making our way home.

"I do not think I shall attempt another egg balintine for some time," Arvi comments.

"It were the shropsy for me," I says, and yawn. I glance to the side at my pal. He looks pretty content, with his eyes half closed as we walk along. I think I'll risk a comment I ain't risked yet and see what happens. "Miss Dlacey sure enjoyed your singing tonight." He looks at me sharp and is sudden real stiff. I probably shouldn't have risked that. Time to change the subject, fast. "I think you shoulda sung some of your own though, like you do at home."

"Those are not for the public hearing," he snorts, and shoots me a warning glare to say, *"and you had better let it stay that way."*

"When you play at home, it's like nothing I's ever heard before, and it's real nice. I think the rest of the kingdom would like it too."

"It is thine rhythms that make the music of such a different quality," he shrugs. I decide not to argue it, as I guess we're both right. Instead, I change the subject again.

"So what had you so all-fired upset you messed up the first notes to the Squire's Song?"

"I was thinking," he says, and I grin at him.

"Truth, I sort of gathered that. About what?" He hesitates a minute. I let him consider it. We get to the thick wooden door set in the south wall and I slip the key in. Not the big old golden key Charlie has, but an iron one Arvi had made for us when we took to living in our little spot outside the castle. The door swings open and we step through. The trees tower over us, shifting a little in the breeze. They look real nice with their summer growth. The squackers are running around cooing to each other in the branches. Our house is just a quarter mile out, where we can still see the castle wall through the trees, but just barely. I gotta smile as we step around the last bend of the path and there it is, settled in its grassy clearing. It's a nice spot to call home.

Quinty is hard at work, protecting our garden from the squackers. One minute she's hissing, her wings raised behind her, chasing a squacker across the grass as it laughs and yells at her, the next she's scuttling up a tree screeching at the critters to stay away. I didn't teach her to protect the garden and our roof tiles, she just does it, and she's good at it too. I don't mind if she eats a few what she catches sometimes. Spoils of war, I figure. Though she doesn't catch too many. The squackers are fast. And they can see in the dark, better than a dragon. Better than anything on Planistah.

"Servant Meagan sent me to the Jaspur

region," Arvi starts sudden and I open my ears[1]. Arvi don't talk about his work much. He drops onto the bench in front of ourn house and I settle beside him. It's nice out here in the sun. It agrees with my full belly and I feel myself kind of going limp, and blinking a little slow. "There was talk of a leermackle in the area." Every muscle tightened in me and the sun sudden don't feel as warm. I stared at the tree across from us. No wonder he slipped out without telling me what he was up to. Everyone knows how a leermackle hunt ends; with the wyrm a little fatter and the hunter only leaving a head behind to bury. "When I arrived the people claimed the beast had gone, for nothing had been heard of it for eight days. The tracks were still clear at the last place it had attacked, however. Turner, it was no leermackle which did that deed."

"What was it then?"

"I do not know. That is what has me so flummoxed!" He flung himself back on the bench, scowling again. He really were flummoxed. "Four people dead, Turner, simply wiped away, one without even his head to remember him by. Something ravaged in that

---

[1] Think, "pricked ears," though their phrase makes more sense.

town. I fear me it was of a much more sinister nature than a mere hungry leermackle."

"What do you think it was?" I rephrased my question. He looked up, watching Quinty come scuttling up and drop on my feet. She curled her wings around my boots and let out a happy sigh that scorched the grass.

"I fear it is of a human origin."

"What, like someone pretending to be a leermackle? How could they manage that?"

"I know not! But... but I fear me if that is the case, the beast has not left, as the townspeople all think. And even if they have, justice needs done for those poor souls bereft of life. An animal thou cannot take justice from, for it slays only out of instinct or hunger. A man slays for altogether different reasons."

"If you're right, it ain't a critter that needs caught, it's a murderer. So, you going to go tell Meagan tonight or tomorrow?"

"Tomorrow. He will be more inclined to listen in the morn." He sudden looked at me, and sat up as if he was ready for a "real discussion," you know. "But what of thee, Turner? How is it with thee?"

"Oh, I's been getting on," I shrugged. "Right now I'm real tired after all that food and flinging and singing, I'm going to bed." I pulled my feet

out from under the snoring dragon and scuttled inside, yawning. That weren't a fake yawn either, I really was worn out. It had been a busy week.

The next day I don't go out much. Just staying around the forest outside our house, or ducking into the castle kitchens for a good snack. I figure Arvi will be around sometime, and I may as well not get him too worried while he is here in town. Or have to answer too many questions. Besides, I really do need to study, what with last week and all, I didn't get as much done as I had meant to. When lunch rolled around, I was settled under a tree, kicking my heels and trying my hand at mathematics again while Quinty tried to find any good leftovers in my pack. I had caught up on most things, and was feeling better about letting Arv look over my books. And wondering where he had gotten himself to. Kleof was still in his stable, so's Arvi hadn't slipped off without me noticing. As I thunk it, I heard Kleof give his huff that says hello, and I hop up real fast and run toward the stable. I doubt Arvi would ride off without at least glancing at my books, but these days I ain't so certain. It seems like I'm not on his mind as

much as other things.

Arvi is there all right, spraying some more of the mud off that still clung to Kleof's hide. His pack was already on the merthyl's back.

But, beside Kleof, my little merthyl bounced around. His name is Ceedric, a green and blond what only reached up to Kleof's shoulder, and has a real happy temperament. His bridal was on. Arvi looks up at me.

"Meagan's sending you back?" I asked, hiding the way my heart leapt at the hope of my merthyl bounding around too.

"No. He had already finished the paperwork for the case, it is closed."

"Then..."

"I took the days allotted to me as a knight of the realm."

"Yourn using your vacation days to go hunt around in Jaspur?" I asked, hiding my smile. Only Arvi. He nodded, then looked up at me again.

"Thou must take thy mathematics along, for thou art well behind in thy bookwork." No, 'Hey Turn, want to come along?' or even, 'Your merthyl needs the exercise, ride with me.' But I don't mind. I let myself grin at him and ran inside awful quick to get a pack ready.

Chapter 3: Screams in the Hillands! or Travel Thereto

We rode easily for two days ere I broached the subject I truly wished to speak of. They were pleasant days. We did not speak often, but both of us enjoyed the company. I had ridden many roads these past three years, most oft alone. It was agreeable to have a friend near. And Turner had grown. Not only in his lanky height (he was but an inch shorter than myself), but in his interests and designs. He seemed closer to manhood than when last we adventured together. In point of fact, it was nigh a year since I hadst time to spend with Turner longer than a mere check of his books. But now we were but two short hours from Peyson and I wouldst have an answer.

"I spoke with Corinth when I was last in Hartsom," I began.

"Truth? So did I," he commented. "Right now I'm a little more concerned about this mud. It stinks! Is this whole place covered in the slimy stuff?" I would not be deterred.

"She told me thou had been escorted back to our quarters by guardsmen. Twice." He did not look at me and gave no sign of what he thought. At least none I couldst read. "I rarely inquire into thy dealings, for I trust thee, Turner. But this is something I wouldst learn of. What happed to bring thee under the scrutiny of the town's lawmen?"

"If you say you trust me—"

"Nay, thou shall not duck the question thus! Trust does not rule out an honest inquiry into thy welfare from a friend. More than a friend, for I stand as brother and elder to thee, and I wouldst know the answer to this question."

"I was helping some friends."

"What friends?" I pressed, as he was disinclined to go on. His hands shot up in a brief helpless gesture, his eyes rolling to the sky. He gave me answer in a swift, annoyed manner.

"Look, even when you ain't around, people need help, see? You ain't been around much this year, and there's been folks down in Hartsom that needed the Protectors of the Innocent, needed the help bad. So me and a few others have formed a sort of...band, to help out every so often."

"Thou have started thine own vigilante gang?" I sputtered.

"Aw, come on Arvi, it ain't that bad. We don't go lopping off heads or nothing. And me and a few of the fellas ain't really a gang."

"What 'fellas'?" I demanded, and knew from

the way he hesitated I would not like the answer. I did not.

"Colly and Creason, Ryles Gotmar, Placky, and a friend of Placky's, Tryle Maurl."

"The young toughs from the dark ways, all some years thy elder, and none reputable."

"They's good hands in a fight, though," Turner said, quiet earnestness in his tone. There was a determined stubbornness behind it and I took a moment to think before I answered. I would speak with him rationally over this, and not drive him further into the foolishness.

"How hast thou handled the villains thou beset? Tell me of it." He glanced at me through lowered lids, as if he tried to guess what my question had behind it. But then he gave a smile and launched into the tale. His gang had done some good work. There were three families reunited that might otherwise have ended in tragedy, and one young fool of a girl who was rescued despite herself. This gang was newly formed, only truly stepping out together in the past two months. Most of it had been successful by mere providential luck, as I had guessed might be the case. Turner was proud of their successes (as well he might be, a lad of thirteen).

But this would not happen again.

I approached the situation with some caution, beginning by merely rephrasing the battle scenes and giving them a new outcome. How wouldst they have handled it if their opponents had reacted differently? Turner bridled. But he did not shut the conversation down. In the end he was honest enough to admit they wouldst have been in difficulties had the opponents truly used their whole strength.

"But they didn't, Arvi, and we got in, got the folks, and got out," Turner insisted.

"Verily, and thou didst good work," I nodded. His mouth snapped shut and he looked at me in surprise. "God used thee and thine companions to rescue those who needed it, and thou acted with bravery. But bravery is not always coupled with sense. This shall not happen again."

"You think just because you order me to–"

"That was not an order," I broke in, my tone dropping and my gaze turning away from his bright eagerness. "I speak with more experience than thou, and thou knows it. These men thou fight have looked on thee as boys, and have not turned their full strength to bear. When they unleash their fury dost thou think thou can withstand it? What will thou do when one of

thine own is wounded and cannot run? Couldst thou leave him there in order to save the rest? Or wouldst thou stay to fight to the last man? If one of the villains managed to gain a member of thine force, he couldst use the boy's screams to torment thee for the rest of thy life, Turner. And the decisions thou wouldst have to make in such a case would ever be thine to haunt thy rest."

"That ain't happened, and likely never will," he said stubbornly. But a good deal of the heat had left him.

"It is but a matter of time. A very short matter of time, I deem, for news of thy doings will have circulated about the haunts and dives of these villains. They shall not look on thee as lightly the next time thou appear. All the force thou hast managed to avoid thus far will be flung against thee. Couldst thou withstand it?" No answer came. "Well?"

"No." He did not snap, as I had expected, but spoke with a hesitant thoughtfulness, chewing the word till it was mangled into several consonants. It changed to a demand. "How sure are you they'll be ready for us this next time we go out?"

"If not this time then the next, or the time after that," I shrugged. "Surely thou knew such good fortune as has followed thee thus far could not last." A sigh heaved from him, and he slumped upon Ceedric.

"I guess so... Actually something in me figured you'd bust it all to pieces when you heard." Turner's gaze lifted to mine and he gave a rueful smile, with no humor behind it. "I guess it was too simple of an answer to the problem for it to work out long."

"I am sorry I have not been there with thee when the need arises." I was somewhat surprised to realize I meant it heartily.

"You've been needed where you were called off to too," Turner shrugged, in another instance of his seeming to have gained a man's way of thinking.

"I do not doubt thy bravery, or even thy skill," I added, suddenly feeling it needed to be said. "Only thy enemies' strength." He nodded that rueful look still upon his features. We rode on in silence for some time. But I needed another answer, before the subject dropped. "Wilt thou cease thy attempts? Turner, I need to hear thee promise to dissolve this gang of yours."

"It ain't a gang, it's a band," he said defensively. Another sigh lifted his shoulders and left them slumped. "All right, yes, yourn has my promise. I'll tell the fellas we gotta' cut

it while we're ahead."

"Good. I thank thee."

The sounds of our merthyls' paws thumping into the oozing mud and then squelching as they lifted them again, overtook the dark afternoon ride. The thump and squelch went on, getting wetter as we traveled deeper into Jaspur.

"Arvi?"

"What?"

"Last year, when you came back from that four-month campaign to stop the raiders in Packston?"

"Well?" I prodded, as he stopped. Though I guessed what he desired to know. Most of me wished he would leave it unasked.

"Tolvy Hume and Bavy Hairk didn't come back with your contingent. Did you have to make some of those decisions, like you just mentioned? I heard your nightmares in the months afterwards," he added softly, as if I might hesitate to answer. But I did not hesitate. The boy should know.

"Yes." My own sigh escaped, rattling through me, and I turned my face away. It was not easy to recall. "Think carefully ere thou turn thy hand to a matter of public service, Turner, whether it be soldier, guardsman, or knight.

The deeds thou accomplish might save many lives, or even rescue the kingdom. But they are like to haunt thee ever after, even if thou know there was no other option to thy hand."

"Maybe I'll stick to Mr. Trosk's workshop," Turner muttered. I smiled at him, and hoped he could read my pleasure in his toils therein.

"He was right proud of thy work the last time I spoke with the man."

"Truth? He don't ever tell me that. Now about this mud, are we going to have to slog through it the whole time we's hunting for this leermackle what ain't a leermackle? Because it's already making me miss my streets, with their sturdy rocks and–"

A fearsome noise interrupted him.

It started as a high, keening wail, that seemed to enter the brain and set my ears ringing at a fever pitch. The next instant the wail was joined by a rumbling howl that vibrated inside my bones. A growl rose and fell between the two, joining them in an awful proof that all sounds came from the same source. Ceedric cowered, pressing against Kleof's side such that our legs were near crushed by his weight. Even Kleof stopped dead still in the road, his ears tying in knots under his chin in his fear. My head spun this way and that, trying to spot the source of the sound, striving with all I was to make out any sign of the beast which made such a horrible din. I could see nothing in the darkness of the afternoon. The howl vibrated and keened around us. But it did not quite surround us, not as described in the books; the call surrounded only the victim of the hunting beast. No, it came from ahead and to the left and seemed to be lessening even as it reached us. The thing (whatever it might be) was leaving. A final high wail rang in our ears, such that the merthyls plunged and backed, shaking their heads piteously to try and be rid of the tormenting sound. The noise cut off as suddenly as it had come. We were left with the darkness, the merthyls' snorts, and our own panting breath.

"Limeny, I thunk my heart was gonna stop, that thing made it shake so bad," Turner gasped. I couldst scarce hear him through the ringing in my ears. But I did hear him put into words what ran through my churning mind. "So much for their leermackle having moved on. Where did it go, and why did it come back again? I think your mystery just got a little deeper, Arvi."

We steadied our merthyls and urged them forward again. Kleof and Ceedric trembled under us, but moved dutifully forward. In another three miles the great trees came in view, showing where Peyson began (every town in Jaspur has a store of the high black trees, for thus the loggers make their business). Turner's eyes grew wide at sight of so large a tree. Then his gaze riveted upon the buildings of the town and a sly look overtook him.

"Say, Arvi, since we's both here, what about tackling different parts of this business?"

"'We are.' What different parts?"

"Well, if'n you're right about this, and it's people making it seem like there's a leermackle around, and not a real leermackle, then there's going to be a human side of it too. And that part's going to be centered in Peyson."

"Thou art slipping in thy grammar, 'if you are,' Turner."

"Did you hear me?"

"I just corrected thy grammar, of course I heard thee."

"Come on, Arv, what do you think?"

"I still do not grasp thy meaning," I answered. He gave a long suffering sigh, turning his eyes heavenward.

"Look, while yourn, all right, *you are,* out slogging through the mud looking for the leermackle what ain't, I'll camp out in town and

see what factlays I can unearth about who's behind the wyrm scare."

"Unearthing things can be a messy job—"

"Not as messy as slogging through all this stinking mud. And if we's, I mean, we are going to split our forces, I was thinking maybe we shouldn't ride in together, like such hot pals."

"Then where will thou sleep? How will thou eat? A lad of independent means in such a town is more suspicious than companion to a knight."

"I'll manage," Turner said airily. I stared upon the boy. A laugh burst from him. Always a ready welcome thing from Turner Hitchley, and it seemed to brighten even afternoon in the mud wastes. "All right, stop your scowling! I'll slip into your room through the window at night so's we can compare notes and all, and I'll get a job to pay for meals. That shouldn't be too hard to scrounge up. Get room number five at the inn, so's I know where you are." I was still doubtful. Turner's schemes did not always enact themselves in reality as easily as they did in discussions. Yet the boy was determined. He turned Ceedric off to the side, between two muddy hills and waved me on with an audacious smile. The memory of the horrendous cry rose in me, and I hesitated. But

then the false tracks came to mind and I turned Kleof toward the town. Whatever haunted this region, and whatever made that sound, it was not a true leermackle. And Turner Hitchley was adept at dealing with anything short of a giant, toothed wyrm.

In another hour, the lights of Peyson shone upon us and Kleof was pacing off the mud onto the cobbles of the town. The streets were not as empty as when first I rode into the town. People crowded the ways, and all seemed to be flowing one direction. After a moment of riding it was obvious they traveled the same path as I did; we were all headed toward the inn. Oft the hurrying people paused to stare up at me, and each seemed surprised, and even glad. For a Jaspur town the gladsomeness at seeing a knight ride in was a worrisome thing. The hulking loggers preferred to solve their own difficulties and looked askance upon those they considered interlopers. The situation must be dire indeed to be glad of a knight. Unless it was as a toy to test their boxing skills upon.

The Resin Inn was packed this day. I pulled Kleof to a stop and slipped inside. Or tried to slip. People made way for me. They cleared a path, and stared in some awe at the muddied trappings of my order.

"Coo, 'ow did Hartsom get 'ere so fast?" someone in the crowd asked.

"That 'as ta be tha swiftest service I 'ave evah 'eard oof!" another called from the back of the room.

"We just sent tha notice this morning, and already ah knight coomes riding in. Which one are you, do we know your name?" a rough clothed lady spoke up from behind the bar.

"I am but a servant sent to thy land," I answered. I had learned it was easier not to give my name if it could be avoided (people grew either shy, angered, or greedy by it). "What can thou tell me of this matter?"

"Only that it's back," the innkeeper growled, as he polished glasses behind his bar. "We need ah wyrm slayah. You don't look like one. Puny, I would call you."

"Sometimes tha short ones still do all right," a woman said doubtfully behind me.

"Short! He is tha size oof my lad oof twelve," another woman called from the left.

"My gal oof twelve is about 'is size," a man called from the back of the room, and a roar of laughter went up.

"Wither away did it go?" I interrupted their critique.

"That is for you to find out," the innkeeper

snorted.

"Where did it strike this last time?" I amended. Silence fell. All eyes turned one direction, toward the center of the great room. I followed the gazes. A large-framed woman sat upon a simple wooden stool. She seemed of middle age, in oft mended clothes but with a more ragged look about her sunken features than her dress. Her shoulders slumped and her breathing came ragged. Her eyes lifted off her feet and focused upon me with difficulty. They were red, near bloodshot, and I couldst see she was on the edge of hysterics. I stepped down into the room, crossed to her stool, and knelt in front of her. After a moment the bloodshot eyes focused on my own, and I knew she recognized my presence.

"Tell me," I said quietly.

"She only went out ta gathah tha eggs," the woman began in a low, lackluster voice. "Then tha noise began. It was everywhere, surrounding tha 'ouse. Tha othah children screamed and screamed in terror. Paulin did not coome back in. Then it stopped. Tha beast's scream, it stopped as suddenly as it 'ad begun. I went out ta look for Paulin. I found…" Her chin began to quiver and anguish took over her stunned face.

"She was standing in tha yard 'olding tha girl's 'ead this morn, when I came by ta check aftah tha noise," a tall, fair-haired man grunted behind the woman's chair. He shifted on his feet, anger, helplessness, and fury seeming to mix in him. His voice when it came was low and husky. "Tha young thing was only fourteen. Ah nice girl, showing signs oof being ah true beauty when once she grew. My son 'ad 'is eye on 'er for ah wife one day. Now she will be no one's except tha dirts." A fist suddenly came down upon a table, just to my left, rattling the crockery four tables away in its ferocity. A giant of a man drew his hand back again, his face livid.

"This must stop! Killing children now... Tha beast must die!"

"Where is this good lady's home?" I asked of the man standing behind the stunned woman. "Couldst thou take me to the site?" In answer he began to lead the way out of the inn. I followed, and the people pressed back, allowing me passage. Some looked upon me gladly, as if the problem already was solved. Most looked as solemn as though they already attended my funeral. Doubtless they thought it certain I shouldst be next upon the beast's list of meals.

It was dark as pitch when we emerged. The blackness of the afternoon pressed upon us, for the moons and their sister stars hid behind thick clouds, which seemed to lower at us, and press down until the very air was thickened by their weight. We each collected a torch from the communal pile, and began on our way. I wondered if Turner had made his way into town yet, or if he still bided in the hill lands waiting for the proper opportunity. I shrugged mentally and continued to follow my silent guide. I had allowed Turner to make his own way, I had no charge of him at this time and must trust to his wily common sense. The cobbles ended and we stepped into the mud wastes. Mounds of mud rose up around us leeching out their stench and barrenness. But by and by my guide stepped into a rounded area where the hills fell away to leave a clearing of sorts. A homestead was scratched into existence here. It was dark enough the light of our two smoking torches lit it well, and I couldst make out what was around us. Patches of grass struggled from the mud, hardly enough to feed the single bony vol ruminating under the shadow of a great hill to our left, while a bevy of hens clucked and cooed to each other in a coop made up of mismatched wood scraps. A small square house (crafted by the same skill and timber as the hen coop) rested just in front of us. This all stood between

two great mud hills, while another glared at the small farm from behind.

But as we turned into the place, what mainly caught my attention was the ground. It was crisscrossed with oval indentions. They ran one just in front of the other, and I nearly had to hop over the widest sections. The peculiar tracks led directly to the hen coop. The ground there was a darker shade of red. Nearly brown. I did not have to study it closely to know what grisly thing had thus dyed it dark. Instead I followed the tracks. They stayed symmetrical even as this thing, whatever it might be, had done its dreadful deed and left the ground so splattered and a mother thus bereaved and traumatized. But the tracks rolled on (I couldst not think of them as running), through the space between the left hill and the one at the back of this scraggly farm. I followed it closely, Kleof thudding faithfully behind me. Our guide stopped at the top of the farm, his eye on the dark stains about the coop.

"I will leave you ta it, Servant," the man growled, as Kleof and I stepped between the hills. Without more farewell he turned and began to walk toward the town. I doused my light, not wishing to be an easily spotted target for miles, then mounted my merthyl. Thus I

began in earnest to hunt this ersatz leermackle.

Chapter 4: A New Ally or Investigations Begin

It looked like a town wide convo was breaking up when I rode into Peyson. But I didn't really think about the huge people passing by me, flowing back from wherever they had come, my mind was on another problem. I should have left Ceedric with Arvi. We could have pretended he was a pack merthyl or something, and then Arv could have put him up in the stable with Kleof. But I didn't think of it, so I has to come riding into town, which makes me change my story some from what it would have been. At first I thought I would play the wandering waif, you know, the orphan boy out to see the world and odd-jobbing his way around. But now I have to account for Ceedric. So when the innkeeper asked me what I wanted stepping into his place, the beginning of my story got changed. Well, how I started it when he asked didn't change, just when they kept digging and I let them find out more. Like this.

"What are you doing in my inn, boy? Only paying customers are allowed 'ere," the innkeeper growled, shaking a glass my way. For a second I really thought he'd chuck it at my head, he seemed that kind of mean bovy. I give him glare for glare and keep coming toward his bar.

"I'm looking for work. Could you use me around the place?" I said.

"Ah nice looking boy like you?" the maid behind the bar asked, doubtful. She don't mean it as a compliment to me, just my things. She cast a glance over my sturdy clothes as she said it, and looked out the window at Ceedric, where he stared in with his nose pressed against the grimy glass, watching what I was doing. He's a real curious type. I hesitated for a minute like I would have if this story was actually me. When I did I saw a boy, about my age, look up at the end of this great room. His face was black with soot from the great fireplace he was cleaning, and real skinny. He were watching like he couldn't decide whether to be interested or upset by my popping in. I didn't fret over it and just launched into answering this maid's doubt.

"Look, my folks were fairly well off. They...they died this winter, and my uncle, he inherited everything except me and my merthyl, and he didn't want either of us, so I'm out making my own way. Seeing something of the world, and getting a little experience odd-jobbing while I'm at it. So, I'll do what jobs you

have. For bed and board for my merthyl and me, and then earn a little extra around town when I have the time."

"I already 'ave an odd-jobbah," the innkeeper growled, waving a hand toward the great fireplace. The boy suddenly remembered himself and started working pretty frantically at getting the ashes out. "He is as lazy as I'm sure you are, and two would be more trouble than it's worth."

"I can cook," I suggested.

"Fancy foods," the innkeeper scoffed. Charlie'd taught me as much as Arvi about cooking, so I could have argued for that one. But I didn't really want to be stuck in a kitchen all day, so I didn't argue it.

"Errand running. I bet your current odd-jobber doesn't have a merthyl. I could get it done twice as fast." The innkeeper hesitated and I could almost see him counting money pieces in his head as he considered it. Faster runs would mean more done, and that ended up meaning money saved. "Room and board for my merthyl in your stable, three meals a day for me, and two guilders," I bargained, cutting out the room for me.

"No coins, one meal. But I'll make it ah good one," he said immediately, and I shook my head. It took a little bit, but we did come to an agreement eventually. This innkeeper had the better part of it, he drove a hard bargain. I was glad I really wasn't on my own and relying on this guy for my way, I don't trust him to keep to even the rotten deal he convinced me to make. The barmaid was glaring at him as he finished, but he don't seem to mind none. Instead he reached under the bar, pulled out a bag of purnaps near as big as me, and heaved it over the bar. It gave such a solid thump when it hit the wooden floor I thought I could feel the boards shake under me. An old, grease-stained map of town comes sailing after it.

"This goes to Meg's Restaurant, at the south end oof tha main road. Hurry up and take it there, then get back 'ere with tha twenty-nine guilders she owes me," the guy growls. Yes, he definitely got the better deal. I grab the map and bag and start to drag the heavy sack out the door. Good thing Ceedric enjoys a challenge.

Ceedric knelt down for me when I got near. I dragged the bag on him, and helped where I could as he staggered up, looking a little surprised at how heavy it was. But he gets excited about doing new things, and especially about helping out when I needed him, so's he didn't really mind. I walked pretty easy at first, but that were just while the lit torches let them in the inn see me. When I knew we were out of sight I started to jog with good old Ceedric huffing at my heels. I didn't want that mean old innkeeper to think I was over eager, see, because then he would toss more stuff onto our shoulders than we wanted to do. I wasn't really here to run his errands. But errand running would give me the chance to get out around folks and strike up conversations, and hopefully learn some things.

I ain't real sure what I should be looking for, so I just look for anything. It will do for a start. I'd gotten Arvi to tell me a thing or two about this Jaspur place on our way down here. I knew just enough to be surprised by the stone streets. And the nice street torches, they worked real well, and looked like some of the fancier spots in Hartsom[2]. And the buildings too, a lot of them were made up of new pine boards, not the old weathered ones I saw peeking out behind

---

[2] Recall in the Dreaded King texts, Mr. Trosk was just beginning experimentation with trapping lightning-inspired energy, and we sent them a little tract on electricity. Now, three years later, they have found out more. They have not made their lightning energy work the same as ours. There is something different in the essential makeup of it, I begin to think, though I don't understand what. I don't think anyone else does either, though the scientists among us pretend to know bits and pieces. However, they have managed a few things, and energy boxes (shorted to e-boxes) are one of them. The energy stored inside does not last long before needing recharged, but it seems to be effective while it is there.

the nice new ones. I trotted closer to the street torches and spied an e-box on every other one, providing the power to that shine on the nice stone streets. Even most neighborhoods in Hartsom ain't got lights powered like that yet.

The restaurant isn't hard to find when we get toward the end of the street. So many folks are there some are seated outside, at little makeshift tables set on the cobbles. I guess that's why they need so many purnaps. I turn around the corner and head down the muddy, stinking alley between this plank restaurant and the plank apartment building beside it. I find the door to the kitchen where I figured it would be, and as I figured it'd be. It's wide open to let the smoke and heat out and the other air in, like most restaurant kitchens.

"Purnaps from the inn!" I called through the door, getting Ceedric to kneel down for me again. As I jerk the bag off I feel somebody coming up behind me, and shift to swing the purnaps toward them. She's a real beefy lady, with whiskers. She catches the bag easy and swings it over her shoulder like there ain't nothing but hen feathers in there. Her clothes are awful nice for a cook... I risk a guess that she's the owner and hold out my hand. "Innkeeper says you owe him twenty-nine

guilders."

"Where is tha usual runnah?" she asks, her voice a little thin and squeaky.

"You mean the other odd-jobber at the inn?" I ask.

"Othah? Since when did that cheapskate hire ah second boy besides Ryam?"

"I'm the new errand runner. Turner Hitchley," I added with a smile, and made to bap her shoulder. She backed up fast, her face wrinkling like I was about to squish a munsom on her.

"How do I know you will take tha money back ta tha inn?"

"I brought you the purnaps, don't I? I'm not a thief," I said, with more heat than I meant it to come out. Everyone in this place seems to be rude and mean. I add another fact that I think might hold for her more than my honesty. "Besides, my merthyl's only a mackleson, if I decided to run off with the money on him I wouldn't get far afore someone catches up to me." She blinks at that, considers a few seconds, then nods.

"Wait," she orders, and goes in. I wait, kind of bouncing on my heels, and hoping she hurries because it stinks out here. But I do some thinking too. Why is the owner out here collecting vegetables when there's so many folks at her place? And twenty-nine guilders for a bag of purnaps? Sure it were a lot of them, but that's still a pile to pay for purnaps. Maybe they's scarce out in this part of the world. I'll have to ask Arvi when I see him next. I was just starting to wonder what Arvi was up to, when the lady comes back out. She tosses a cloth bag what's almost the same size of my head at my face, and spins around back into the kitchen without even waiting to see if I catch it or it breaks my nose. I do catch it, right toward the top. The bottom half swings around and clips my ear so's I stagger and see stars for a few seconds. I rub it a little as I clamber up on Ceedric, working hard at not being real mad at these rude people.

I head back, and push Ceedric to a run. That innkeeper's one to have spies at the restaurant to keep track of his money bags. I'd better not linger from here back to there. The cobbles pound under us as Ceedric really likes to run. He ain't all that fast, but he has a good time at it, and so do I. The folks on the street glare some, but we don't care and just keep thundering on past, straight toward the inn. It don't take us long.

When we round the last corner, Ryam the

other odd-jobber is in the street. He's slapping his hands together to get the last of the ash off as he walks back toward the inn from dumping the stuff in the alley. I just get a glimpse of him though, because afore he can hardly take a step, three big fellas, probably sixteen or so, sudden step out of a door and come at him. They's wearing a look I know well. It's what Gaully and Beckmar used to wear when they came at me, or Big Yim and some of his crowd. One shoots a hand out and slams it into Ryam's chest. It sends him staggering back into the alley. I seen Ryam's hand close around a board lying loose beside the building and swing it up, then he's out of sight, and the other three disappear into that alley.

I jerk Ceedric toward the alley. But I don't slow him down none. We thunder in with Ceed's nose flap high and his ears wiggling. Before we's on them I get another glimpse of the situation, in the smoky dim light of the inn's back kitchen torch. There's a bruise with splinters embedded in it on the biggest boy's face, where I can see Ryam's got a good shot in. But there's also a broken board on the filthy ground in this place, fury on all the big ones' faces, and the odd-jobber down in the muck with the three just starting in proper on him.

Ceedric rams into the one on the left, with all the force of his run behind it. That big one goes smashing into the side of the inn like to shake the wall. As he slumps to the ground in a daze, I swing the money bag off my shoulder. I slam it hard on the biggest one's head, where he stands with his boot pulled back ready to smash it into this Ryam. He goes down without a sound, just folding up into the muck. But I's already dropping off Ceedric in front of the last one and hardly notice. The last one don't have a chance to even think, I make sure of that. My foot shoots out. One pleason kick brings him down onto the mud, whimpering a little and looking really shocked. People don't expect fighting like the pleason from someone my age. At first Arvi frowned at street moves like that, calling them dirty. But then he changed his mind and said whatever gets it over fast and you out of there is fair game. I taught him a move or two after that.

The one Ceedric rammed staggers up. He's doing everything he can to keep back the groans from all the bruising he has now, and leaning fairly heavy on that wall.

"Oops," I said, real innocent. Ryam clambers to his feet, his fists balled. "My merthyl got a little carried away, looks like. And that made me drop my bag, and limeny, looks like I accidentally kicked one of you when I fell off my merthyl." I shook my head, my eyes real wide and innocent as I look at the big guy next to the money bag. "I think maybe you had better drag your friend out of the muck, he might drown in all that." I patted Ceedric's shoulder as I finished. He danced a little closer to the two of them still awake, snorting and huffing like a mad critter. I knew he were just having a grand old time with all this excitement, but I guessed maybe these two don't know merthyls that well. Sure enough, they eyed my noisy dancing critter like he were the latest crossbow aimed at their heads, grabbed their pal by the arms and staggered on out of the alley. I let myself grin as I hauled up the bag again. Ryam were eyeing me. When he turned his face to the torch, the fire from the fight reflected still in his brown eyes. We were about the same height I noticed.

"Looked to me like those bovys were waiting for you," I commented.

"They tend to know when Mulk the innkeeper sends me out," he kind of growled.

"What'd you do to make them have it in for you?" I asked as he picked up his hat.

"Does anyone in Jaspur need a reason to fight?"

"That wasn't exactly a fight," I found myself saying. He looked up at me, the fire still in his eyes.

"It would have been if my board hadn't broken."

"Truth, yourn right about that," I grinned at him. Then I reached out fast and bapped his shoulder afore he could back out of it like the restaurant owner. "Turner Hitchley, fellow odd-jobber and bag dropper." He stares doubtful at me again for a minute. Then he kind of gives a shake, and his stiff defensiveness dropped off. It left him just looking a little tired and dirty as he bapped me back.

"Ryam Kicklesmight, wielder of the broken board," he says, and I laugh. He points sudden at my ear, what still throbs a little. A crooked smile cuts over his face, making him sudden look smart and a little wily, like anything at all might come out of his mouth. "You missed the bag when Mistress Jackim tossed it."

"Didn't miss, just caught it in the wrong spot," I said as I turned to make my way back to the inn. "I could have used a warning about that. I had better go hand it over before the innkeeper sends a bevy of lawmen on my–" Ryam's hand shoots out and grabs my shoulder to pull me to a stop.

"You are no odd-jobber," he says. "And you didn't come from well to do parents, unless they made their way up from the streets and kept most of the tenants of their old life."

"Oh?" I says, not saying either way. He gives that crooked smile again and I decide I'm going to like him.

"'Bovys'? And a kick like that! Not everyone knows moves such as that one. I wouldn't mind learning it myself. You gave Mulk glare for glare this afternoon and he backed off, I have never seen anyone make that happen! Also, if you don't mind my mentioning it, you have very interesting scars." He traced one hand over his cheek toward his ear, and the other hand along the back of his neck where one of my whip scars sometimes shows above my collar. "It marks you as a very interesting character. But not a sheltered son of the nobler class. What are you really doing here?" It were my turn to hesitate. Finding what I needed to find was going to take all the sneakiness I had. Though I guess an insider's view might help too...

"Mind if I ask you the same thing?" I said, deciding not to answer him just yet. "You don't talk like yourn from Jaspur. And if you don't mind the comment, you aren't quite built like the rest of them either."

"Weedy, aren't we, the two of us?" Ryam nods, looking rueful, and I grinned at him.

"Only compared to the Jasper folks. So why are you here working for the mean old Mulk?"

"He is a dastardly villain isn't he? The man knows exactly when those three are going to be about looking for me, and that's always when he chooses to send me on the little annoying errands that get me in their way."

"You are ducking the question," I smiled at him. He shrugged.

"No more than you. But then my answer isn't a secret. And if you ask someone else in town their answer might not be as accurate as mine, so I suppose I may as well tell you myself. My parents moved here when I was four. They came from Packston, for my da to do some miner work in the area. Ten years we have lived here, but we will always be the outsiders, only visitors compared to the rest of the town. I wanted to be a teacher."

"No fooling?" I asked, a little surprised. He nods, moving over to Ceedric to get a better look at my merthyl. And to hide his expression I think, afore he goes on with it.

"Three years ago Mother and Da sent me off to Neeples. I liked it there, though I missed all of them. I have five younger siblings, which

makes school life something of a quiet bore[3]."

"Now you're back here..." I prodded, curious by now. He keeps petting Ceedric, not looking at me.

"Da disappeared last year. I came back to help as I could."

"Oh. It's real hard to lose them, isn't it?" I asked, kind of soft, my mind on Grams. He looks at me then, his sharp look back on.

"Was that part of your story true?"

"Sort of," I shrugged. "My mum and da are dead all right. Now, I had better get this in to Mulk or we might both find ourselves in front of the judge accused of attempted thieving."

"You already know him well," Ryam muttered and I smiled at him as we shifted toward the inn. I hadn't learned too much this afternoon. But at least it seems I had made a friend. Things like that tend to come in handy.

---

[3] Teachers in Asesthwesian culture have a higher regard in society than they do here, hence Turner's surprise at meeting someone daring to try and attain the high learning that goes into the job. There are particular schools setup to teach those aspiring to such a lofty post, Neeples is one of the distinguished ones.

Chapter 5: Near Death in the Mud Wastes or The First Encounter

The trail led on smoothly. I couldst follow it even in the dark, for the indentions showed in deeper blackness than the rest of the land we rode through. The black shapes of hills rose around us, their outline just visible against the darkened sky. Kleof's paws splattered and slucked as he sloughed through the mud, steadily cantering on. We were both of us splattered high with the stinking stuff. Even my cloak hood failed to keep the mud from my face. It splattered me in dots and streaks, and I had nothing clean about my person to remove it. We rode on in stoic silence, ever watching the deep indents. This thing headed to the south, away from Peyson, deeper into the mud wastes where the trees could not set their roots, and even the grass had difficulty latching on. There was naught around us but the thud of my merthyl and the occasional wet oozing sound as a stack of mud broke from one part of a hill and slid down to create a new part. Still the tracks led on.

A clap of thunder rolled overhead. It came deep and echoing from hill to hill, ominous with

the dread promise it carried. Rain in this muddy place would fill these indentions and wipe away the trail as if it had never been. I prayed the rain would hold back at least until the sun rose. Then I couldst mount a hill and spy out the direction of these tracks for miles, and it would only be an inconvenience if the tracks themselves were wiped away. Again came that clap of thunder. I pushed Kleof to a faster pace, though I dared not press him too hard. One slip in this mud couldst mean a broken leg. Even his fifth limb wouldst do little against such a catastrophe. But my merthyl ploughed on steadily, sturdy fellow.

It was nearing the last hour of the afternoon dark when the first of the raindrops fell. It landed upon the top of my head, so large and cold I couldst feel it even through the thick black material of my hood. The next splashed upon the back of my hand as it pressed against Kleof's neck feathers for warmth. I shuddered at the icy touch. After that the drops came in swift succession. It promised to become a torrent within but a few moments unless God called it back up to the heavens. The hills still rose around us in their monstrous black shapes, but as the raindrops landed we could hear the oozing slides and drops increase exponentially.

Losing the tracks might be the last of our troubles. Losing ourselves in the midst of this desolate, shifting mud was more of an urgent worry. It was not the difficulty of finding our way back, that would not be hard. It was the real possibility of riding too close to one of these hills and becoming trapped in one of the numerous mud slides. I had no wish to be immortalized for posterity as a fossil knight.

Kleof plowed on, never tiring in his dogged tracking. The rain increased with each moment till it was a torrent indeed. The blackness of the afternoon began to give way to the denser, deadlier blackness of a Jaspur rain (in all its icy fury and oxygen-deprived density). The tracks ahead of us were as indiscernible as those behind now. Even our own tracks were washed away as soon as they were made. I began to ruefully calculate our path back toward the road, striving to see through the icy torrent such that I might make out the shape of the hills about us. The pounding of the rain streamed into my face, my ears, all of me. It was numbing, and too loud to even shout above. Yet there was a noise that couldst pierce it.

A high keening wail cut through the pounding of the rain. It seemed to cut through my chest into my very heart. The noise bounced

from hill to hill and vibrated in my mind till my ears rang at a fever pitch. A deep rumbling growl joined it, and my insides shook as a mold of vol's fat. My heart leapt and jolted at the intensity.

The cry came from every side. It surrounded us.

Kleof stopped where he stood, his feet bunched under him and his head ducking toward his feet. I did not press him on. The fearsome noise of the murdering beast encircled us. We wouldst not leave this day without a fight, whatever might make this call. Illustrations of leermackles rose in my mind as the rain pounded and the beast's call wailed and bellowed in a ceaseless cacophony about me. The bulbous brown body, rippling in its own fat. Six feelers reaching off its face. The pinchers at the end of each feeler prepared to grip a man and drag him toward the round eyeless hole, lined with three rows of serrated teeth, which made up the face of the monster. For that instant I wished I had carried my spear out hunting with me. (Even so strong a blade as Peace wouldst be little use against a leermackle's leathery hide.) But I did not allow myself to live in such monstrous dreams.

Peace leapt from his sheath into my hand.

Her bright silver blade shimmered even in the rain fall. At the first hint of the growl uniting the rumbling and the keening whine, my feet were freed from the stirrup feathers and I dropped to the ground. Mud caught at my boots and enveloped them up to my ankles. The red muck churned and ran with the rain, striving to drag my feet from me with its pull. The wail grew to a fever pitch, till I couldst hardly bear the sound. I sensed Kleof plunging and fighting in his distress. My heart pounded such that the pain of it grew with each moment in the awful noise. It was the hunting call.

I stumbled forward, away from Kleof, ducking low and willing my boots to move against the mud. Something in me declared this thing sought my life, not my war merthyl. If I distanced myself from Kleof he wouldst be less likely to become a target. The rain blinded me more than any absence of the sun. The ceaseless downpour made it impossible to make out anything of the world around me. My cloak hood was soaked through and gave me no protection against the icy cold. Mine eyes closed against the frozen rain and I stumbled forward in blackness, desperately seeking the source of the horrible noise.

But it surrounded me.

I couldst gain no bearing of the enemy. That hated call rang all about me, ringing in my mind and shaking my guts such that clear thinking became impossible. I focused on the rain, distancing myself from the debilitating, bestial scream. I must have my wits about me. The rain pounded, freezing, heavy, making breathing difficult and miring the already muddy ground. I stopped running. The rain pounded into me and the mud rolled around my feet, clutching at me and striving to draw me farther down into it. But if I did not move, perhaps this thing wouldst be as blind to my whereabouts as I was to it. A true leermackle wouldst be little hindered by rain and blackness, its feelers wouldst have had me ere now. But this couldst not be real.

The hideous call rang around me and doubt ate at my aching heart. I stood gasping, striving painfully to breathe against the pounding rain, the cold, and the furious beat of mine own heart.

Nothing I had ever come across couldst be capable of making this horrible hunting call, this scream that debilitated its victims by mere sound, before the creature moved in for the kill. Was it moving toward me at the moment? Something drew me here, knowing I wouldst follow their tracks. Something made that call, the horrendous noise which debilitated my merthyl and kept me helpless in this mud and rain and dark. But a true leermackle wouldst have already moved in for the kill.

I turned me slowly about, searching the darkness with every sense alert. There was not much to use. My eyes were blinded by rain and dark, my hearing assaulted by the wild scream of the leermackle (nearly unbearable in its volume and quality). Yet there was something... something out there. Waiting. Watching. All of my hunter and soldier's instincts told me so. I strove to find it, to tell me where this thing was. Or what it was. The rain poured, the mud churned (striving to lock down my feet), and the scream went on and on. My mind began to spin as the scream kept on, hammering inside of me. It seemed as if the ringing in my ears took over the whole of my body, shaking me to my core. The laboring beat of my aching heart became irregular, and breathing was difficult.

The rain stopped.

In an instant the pounding, icy downpour was called back to the heavens and the scene changed. The scream bit out at us in all its fury. I staggered back, grinding my teeth in an effort to drive the sound out. I sensed Kleof was maddened, plunging and crying, as he tried to be rid of the horrible sound. But also in that instant the instinct that I had clung to screamed at me. The something saw me. It was coming.

I flung myself to the mud, rolling to the left and desperately clutching my klackmen to myself. Something thin moved the air over me, where I had been standing but a moment before. I was up again in a moment, my eyes open in slits, striving to pierce the darkness with my blurry vision. A slight movement in the air came from my left. Peace drove up, my arms becoming rigid. My klackmen rang as something connected with his blade. The force of it drove me back, my boots sliding through the mud and my arms near numb at the impact.

A sliver of silvery moonlight landed on the muddy hill to my right. The sliver grew till it encompassed me, and then all of the scene. The first moon rose and her light filled the scene with what seemed intense luminosity after such a black hunt. The clouds rolled back and the moons shone forth in all their glory. I turned me in a swift circle, Peace held stubbornly in front of my neck. Nothing couldst be seen except wet sliding mud and my poor distressed war merthyl.

The growl tying the horrendous scream

together cut off. Then the rumble shaking my gut and causing my heart such distress ceased. The keening wail went on for yet another few seconds, and it seemed interminable. Then it too ceased. Silence fell (excepting Kleof's pained moans and the ceaseless movement of the settling mud). My ears rang at a fever pitch. But my mind began to calm itself again. Save for a monstrous headache. Yet my head was still attached to my shoulders and thus able to ache. For that I couldst be truly thankful. The sensation of being watched, of the something there with me, also left. Whatever it was did not wish to be out even in the light of the moons. I let Peace's point drop and heaved a long shaky breath. My heart still quavered in me and my head pounded. But I was alive. A true leermackle wouldst never have left me alive.

I was in no state to ponder it long. And Kleof, poor fellow, was incapable of carrying me farther on the hunt, to see if there were yet tracks left by the ersatz wyrm. We would hie back to town, in whatever order we couldst muster. I grimaced as I stumbled to my merthyl and began to rub Kleof's neck and gently untie his ears, attempting to sooth his distress. It wouldst be a long way back this night. I prayed me the thing hunting us was truly gone.

Chapter 6: The Mystery Deepens or Regrouping

ou 'ad bettah coome back soonah with this load then you did with tha last," Mulk growled. If I were a little closer, I think he would have reinforced his orders with a clout from the wooden mug he was holding. I was liking this Mulk less every time I was around him. But I just grabbed the sack of potatoes and began to drag it out to Ceedric. It was heavy, real, real heavy. Even more than the last two bags of purnaps. Mulk must have a stranglehold on all the vegetable suppliers in the area, or something, because why else were these loads full enough to weigh as much as they did? Ceedric didn't seem to mind.

We made it to the mill and back quick enough. But I wasn't keen on getting another job tossed our way, we'd already delivered three bags of purnaps and two of potatoes, and they was all real big loads. The night sun was well on its way across the sky. It were time to give Ceedric a rest. Truth, I wouldn't mind a rest myself. But that did pose a bit of a problem; Arvi hadn't come back yet, so he hadn't rented a room, so I couldn't go sneaking in a window and settle into the nice warm. I guess I could bed down with Ceedric if I did it careful, so no one saw me. But the tightwad Mulk would think of that and charge in to see if I were there. I weren't going to settle in one of these alleys, too much muck to get off myself in the morning.

I pulled Ceedric to a stop in front of the inn and dropped off, feeling real tired. I opened the door, tossed the bag of money onto the bar in front of this Mulk, and quick closed the door again. I didn't want another job tonight. It hadn't done me any good, anyway. Everyone in this town was suspicious and ornery, no one would talk to me. They wouldn't tell me the time of day without some real wheedling, there weren't a chance I could get them to tell me about the beast. I was beginning to be especially glad I had made a contact of Ryam. He might be the only one I could ask about things.

As I turned Ceedric toward the stable building, he stopped and lifted his head, staring up the street. A huff of greeting came from him and I quick looked where he was staring. Kleof was padding up the street. I hear a sigh slide from me as I see Arv safe and whole, and the relief surprises me. I guess maybe a part of me wondered if this leermackle really was a leermackle. I know the odds for hunter and hunted for a real one. But Arvi came riding

back, as always. No, I corrected myself as they
got closer, not quite as always. The mud was
caked so thick over both of them I thunk they
must have brought near a whole hill into town.
Arvi's eyes was closed in slits and he was
slumped as he rode. Kleof's ears were flat and
down, I noticed, and he kept swinging his head
this way and that, like he were watching for
something and real nervous about finding it. I
ain't never seen Kleof nervous. They get to the
inn and pull to a stop by the door, almost like
it's a goal theys been trying to hit afore they
collapse. Arvi goes slow as he shifts off Kleof
and his eyes are almost all the way closed.
When he drops to the ground his legs near give
out on him and for a second he has to hold
himself up by Kleof's feathers. I shift over to
him quick. But then I seen Mulk staring out
through one of the windows. I stayed in
character.

"Want me to look after your merthyl, sir?" I
asked. Arvi blinks at me through slitted lids.
Then he grunts, waves Kleof toward me and
steps inside the inn, moving careful, like he
doesn't want to shift his head any more than he
has to. I run a hand down Kleof's neck,
murmuring to him. I feel him give a shiver what
says he's calming down just being here and

knowing me. I move him to the stable's sprayer, still talking gentle to him, and get most of the mud off afore it can cake on proper. Then I pull open the stable doors and Ceedric and Kleof both follow me in. Musty hay and dust motes dancing in scattered light beams were what I noticed most about the place. And that it were empty. There weren't any other critters stabled here. I led the way toward the stalls, both merthyls following me contented like.

"Why are you here?" someone hisses, popping up from behind a stall door. His head was so close to my ear I feel his breath from the words. I fall back with a little yell, one hand automatically shooting toward the dagger in my boot, what Mrs. Hartsom has been teaching me how to use. Then I register who it is.

"Shut it, Ryam, don't hop out at folk like that!"

"Sorry," he says, and sort of looks it. He opens the stall door and slips out, and I see it has fresh hay and water in it. Ceedric and Kleof both slide in, content to share the place so long as they both get a drink of that nice clear stuff.

"I thought you went home hours ago," I says.

"I did. But I couldn't sleep because you are a mystery, and mysteries keep me awake. You might say thank you for my getting a merthyl

stall ready for you."

"Thank you."

"You are quite welcome. Now why are you here?" he asked, quick like, as if he just couldn't stand not asking any longer. I stared at him a second. Aw, why not.

"I want to know about this beast that's been plaguing the place," I said, as I move to see if I can find the merthyl food. Ryam grins and does a little hop as he follows at my heels.

"I knew it when I saw you with the knight's merthyl! The giant beast knows you, so you must know his owner. Are you his groom?"

"What?"

"Maybe his personal servant? Or his note runner!"

"Not likely," I grinned at him. "Naw, this knight's my... guardian, I guess you'd call him." Even after three years I still ain't quite sure what to call Arvi. "And my pal. So when he was sent down here after the leermackle, I came too. I figured maybe we could learn more if it didn't seem like I was with him, you know, because folks might talk to me when they might not to a knight."

"No one talks to strangers in Peyson."

"I'm gathering that."

"Wait, why do you want people to talk to

you? The leermackle is out in the mud wastes. And if information about the beast is actually needed to hunt it down, I do think people will talk to your knight," Ryam says, watching me measure out merthyl food.

"He thinks there might be a human part to it too," I admit, heading back with two bags of good food. Ryam hops at my heels, real excited.

"Honestly? Could someone train a leermackle? But that would mean—" He stops so sudden his word gets cut off in the middle. I turned around and found him looking a little pale and real solemn. "That would mean Da wasn't just eaten... He was murdered."

"You think that's what happened to him? I heard the beast didn't show up until a few months ago."

"I thought you said you hadn't gotten anyone to talk to you?"

"I can still listen."

"Oh. Well, you wouldn't hear about the beast getting my father. But that is what Mother and I have always thought. Da just didn't come back one day," Ryam says, his voice solemn and a little soft. "He was working on something to the south, in the mud hills, and he hadn't said what it was. Except that he was very excited, and thought it would be his mark upon the world, a gift to all of Planistah. The money was good, and in a letter to me he said it 'was something new, unseen by the above-dwellers,' which is what he called non-miners. And one day he just didn't come back. It was about three months later that the first vol disappeared. Then the livestock started being found slaughtered or just gone. Another two months and the first scream was heard, about when Henison, the miller's son, died. That's when people started thinking it was a leermackle."

"Why did it take them so long to send for a wyrm slayer?"

"It is Jaspur," Ryam shrugged. "If a person can't solve his own problems he is considered a weakling. Which is just silly. I wish someone would solve our problems." The last was muttered just to himself, like he had forgotten I was even there. I dropped the food in the bins, watched Ceedric and Kleof tuck in, real pleased with it, then turned to Ryam.

"I'm sorry you have to share your post with me for a bit. I won't be here long at least, and Mulk ain't paying me any real money for it. Does he actually pay you?"

"A little. Enough for us to get by, added to what else we have. And some vegetables sometimes."

"What is it with these vegetables?" I asked on an impulse. "The delivery bags are so heavy Ceedric has trouble lifting them! Where do they come from, and why does he have so many of them?"

"Pickter, one of the larger loggers, used to make those deliveries. He is probably hunting for you with great fury by this point."

"Truth? I'll have to watch for that. Say, Ryam, when you left was the town... Well, spiffed up as much as it is now? With the cobbled roads and real nice street torches and new buildings and all?"

"No. That started just about a year ago, according to Melsa, my sister." Ryam was looking real thoughtful now. I felt the same. But Arvi's strained face was also in my mind, so I don't prolong the convo out here in the stable. Instead I went for the dust and started to rub down Kleof so's I could get in to Arvi and see how he was surviving. Ryam watched me for a minute, then asked a little hesitant if he could help. He had a grand time dusting up Ceedric for me. He asked if maybe he could bring a sibling or two by to meet my critter, and I said sure, a little distracted like, and he skipped off home, and I slipped out the back window. That one butted right up against the inn. I had

scoped out the place earlier today and knew where room five was. So long as Arvi remembered to ask for the right number, we were all set.

I pulled a pair of gloves out of Arvi's packs, slipped them on, slung the rest of the packs over my shoulder, and hopped onto the window sill. The wall was uneven and packed with handholds. Knotholes, tree bowls, roughened edges, the pine boards were a real easy climb. I scurried up fast, pushed the shutters open, and dropped into the room. I landed crouched, ready to jump back out in a hurry if Arvi hadn't taken this room after all. The shadows played over the place, but the sun streaming in the window was enough to see by. A food cart rested near the door, dinner was already up. Plain wood furniture, moderately clean, two beds, and only one person.

Arvi splayed on his stomach on one of the beds, wet from washing the mud off and wrapped in his spare cloak. His head was shoved under the pillow. I stood up, closed the shutters quick, and stepped over. I don't see no wounds bleeding out all over the sheets. Or even real bruising. I checked again to make sure the room was pretty dark (I'd been banged around enough to know how it was with a bad

headache) then reached up and pulled the pillow off. Arvi groaned, turned on his side, and flung an arm over his face.

"So what happened to you?" I asked, keeping it quiet. Even quiet, Arvi still winced and shifted his arm enough to glare at me. I pulled the dinner cart closer, dropped onto the other bed, and raised an eyebrow at him.

"The beast's scream is enough to drive a man out of his senses," Arvi muttered. "Did thou bring up my clothes?" I toss the packs toward his bed. He shifts up slowly, and told me about his afternoon as he finishes cleaning all the mud off'n himself. I start to open up the dishes and shove things on a plate as I listen. But truth, my mind's mostly on Arvi's tale. It's quite the story! Soon he's plopped on the bed again, reaching for the plate. The cooking here was plain, but there was plenty of it at least. Lots of purnaps and potatoes, I noticed. He laid Peace on the bed beside him as he finished the story and started to eat. I let out a whistle. There was a nick in the klackmen, so deep it near went all the way through the fourth blade to bite into the center ring.

"Whatever it was what near took your head, it was plenty strong and sharp," I said.

"This I know," Arvi says, and goes on

scarfing hen meat.

"Here's something you may not know. The town only started fixing itself up, with the cobbled roads and nice street torches and all, a year ago. And there's been five murders, not four."

"A young girl, I know, I was informed when I rode into town."

"A girl? No, I hadn't heard about her. That makes six then."

"Six? Who are thou speaking of?"

"A miner what disappeared a year ago. His son works here and we've struck up a convo or two. Well, truth is he already knows what I'm actually doing here and is excited to help out."

"A miner? That makes a logger, a miller's son, a traveling grocer, a grandfather, a young lady, and a miner. All of different ages and different vocations. With an ordinary murder one would hunt for a connection to try and spot the one who would do the deed."

"Maybe. But really you follow the money. It will take you to who yourn looking for every time. Behind every crime is the money."

"Not every crime," Arvi muttered, then went on fast so's I wouldn't ask about it. "A link wouldst help our case. But I do not see how these different persons couldst be connected."

"Maybe we just don't have all the factlays yet," I say, reaching for the last of the bread. "There has to be something. The miner was working on something new, he told Ryam, to the south of Peyson."

"The girl that was slain was merely gathering eggs. And she was to the north. However, the logger, who first I was called forth to avenge, had been traveling the south road for three days, carrying messages to the loggers there. I do not know the others' tales."

"I'll keep asking around, maybe if I can learn more about these folks, it will tell me what we're missing. Say Arvi, are purnaps and potatoes scarce out here?"

"What?"

"Are purnaps and potatoes scarce in Jaspur."

"No," he said, staring at me like I were a few leaves short of a pot. "They are easy crops to grow in all regions, and as the seeds are not costly, are a favorite of the common people."

"Thanks, Arv. It's nice having you around again, I've missed my walking encyclopedia."

"If thou art done with thine random questions, I will gain some sleep before the night is fully over," Arvi almost grumps. He flops back on the bed and throws his cloak

around himself again.

"What are you going to do? When the night is over, I mean," I asked as I climbed up higher on the other bed. It were pretty soft for such a grumpy inn owner.

"Search again for the ersatz leermackle. It is in my mind that the sun might show me things the night could not."

"All right, but don't go losing your head over it."

"Thine puns are not appreciated tonight," Arvi grunted, and I smiled as I flopped back on the pillow. I wouldn't tell him it wasn't all a pun. Arvi could handle it, even if it did turn out to be a real leermackle. Of course he could. That's what I told myself as I curled on that bed and let sleep start to find me, and tried to shove the picture of his nicked klackmen out of my mind.

Chapter 7: In the Wake of the Beast or Tracking

I found Kleof hearty and well when I strode into the stables next morning. I saw signs of Ceedric having bedded with my war merthyl, but Turner and his beast were nowhere to be found this morn. If not for his rumpled bedclothes and the dinner mess left behind I wouldst be inclined to think his presence last night and our conversation but a dream conjured up from my sickened head. I had not had such an ache as that since my last concussion. And then my heart had not been ill as well. This morn the aches persisted, but were mild enough to but cause me discomfort. Kleof moaned in greeting and opened his stall with his nose flap as I neared. It seemed he was well and eager to be off. In but a few short minutes we were pounding along the northern road, searching again for the farm where the tracks had begun.

It was not difficult to find the spot, for it was between two large hills, in such an open place as I had not seen elsewhere in this area. As we neared, the sounds of children's voices came to me. They were plenteous, but not the boisterous noise I had come to associate with children after

spending time in the Trosks' company. (The eldest two Trosks were occasional hunting companions of mine, when I couldst spare the time, and we usually took our findings to their home to feast upon with the family. Those were boisterous times indeed.) These voices were solemn, subdued. One I thought wept. I slowed Kleof considerably before I turned into the farmyard.

A large family gathered there, about a newly laid stone. The father had been gone taking their meager crops to the Jaspur market, I had been informed, and was returned but that morning. Now he stood with his haggard wife and their seven children. Seven living children, I silently amended. Their eldest lay under a stone. She had only stepped out to gather the eggs for her sibling's dinner, as a dutiful daughter. I turned Kleof away from the scene, my heart sick within me.

Whatever caused this ersatz leermackle, it must be stopped.

I rode around the back of the great hills and joined the place where I had first begun the trail, where the farm ended and the bare muddy places truly began. There were no roads here, no farms, no tol fields. Nothing but the rounded hills stretching out for miles upon miles. To be ambushed here would be dangerous indeed. Almost certainly fatal. The desolation and solitude brought to mind the barren twists in my home region. Some places a man should hesitate to enter, unless in dire straits.

There were no tracks this day, of course. The rain had washed the land clear, causing the mud to run such that it settled into new formations and smoothed out the ground. Yet I couldst find the starting place with ease. From there it wouldst not be too hard to trace the general direction. Where we had been stopped by the beast's screams, the land was split into three hills spaced in a perfect triangle. It was not a foolproof way in which to search out the spot, but it wouldst have to serve. I prayed God wouldst see fit to guide our way, for I had only that memory and the direction in which we had ridden, and that through a land which looked as similar as two blades of grass.

The morning sun climbed steadily, and had reached its zenith when I drew Kleof to a stop. A hill rose before me, and two others on my right and left. They were still oozing from the rain last night, and not a single track showed in the stinking mud. Yet this was where we were beset yesterday. If I needed confirmation of my own knowledge, Kleof gave an uneasy bellow,

and began to freeze. I laid a hand upon his head, stroking the soft feathers and murmuring in his ear. We would not be assaulted again. Not in the light of the sun, unless my surmise of this beast was entirely false. Kleof gradually untensed under my hand and I was able to ride him around to the other side of the hill forming the top of the triangle, where the memory of yesterday would not haunt him. His great head tossed in a grateful moan but as I dismounted to the mired ground I noted his nose flap was still lifted high. He did not care for this place. I silently agreed with the sentiment as I unclasped my cloak and tossed it over Kleof's saddle feathers, to keep it from trailing in the stinking mud. No need to launder it again.

My boots sank deep with each step, and it took a great effort to lift them from the gripping clay each time I moved. But I gave it no heed and began the climb to the top of the hill. It was a wearisome task. I slid down near as far as I stepped up each time I moved, and was ever on the verge of landing flat in the mud from a spill. But I needed to see what might be found at the top and kept on. I was blowing hard as I crested the hill, for my heart was still weakened with the trauma it suffered yesterday. Verily, what a scream that was! To wound a man from the inside out, with naught but sound? Such a hunting method was monstrous indeed, if not from a monster in truth.

Nay, but it was from a monster. If not a true wyrm, then it was twice as monstrous; if it came from man's hand the thing was evil. A beast could not be called evil, not truly, for the creatures only act out of instinct, as they have been created. In that they are more upright than any man, for we do not act as our Creator made us to be. Not one of us can claim even the same righteousness as a beast. The animals do what they are made to. We do the opposite. Man is made to honor and serve his God, and we come from our mother's wombs already shaking our fists in the face of the Creator, willing to do any manner of evil in contrariness to His commands. It is only man who can claim the horror of traitorous evil.

Of a sudden my boot sunk deep into the mire and I pitched forward. The mud seemed to reach up and grab for me. My leg bent unnaturally as I splayed into the muck, my hands spraying it far as they landed with a wet slap. Mud splattered up to cover my face. I spluttered and spit as I slid forward, striving to extricate my foot from whatever it had embedded itself in. It was a worthy reminder that I shouldst keep my mind upon my work and not the abstracts while I was in the midst of these barren wastes. My leg came out with a slucking pop. I nearly slid off the far side of the hill at the sudden lessening of resistance. I was vaguely glad Turner was not here to laugh at my discomfiture. But at the same instant, I had the urge to fling a mudball at his head and let a mock war begin (I was as muddied as I couldst be and it had been long since I had a companion near to enjoy such harmless entertainment). My left leg was heavy with the mud clinging to it, and already striving to stiffen as the sun beat upon the clay. It was harder than I expected to stagger to my feet and back to the top of the hill, where I had plunged to my muddied ignominy.

There was a hole embedded here. (I feel a fool for writing it, for of course there was, it had swallowed my leg. But it must be said, that I might make the thing clear.) It was a deep black scar upon the hilltop, cavernous, and shaped something as a half moon. That was curious indeed. No animal that I was aware of made a hole in such a shape as this. I began to cast about, driving my boots and hands into the ground, too muddied already to care about the stench and muck steadily splattering me. In places it began to dry, creating a sort of clay shell upon my person. After two minutes of casting about I found the second hole. It was shaped like unto the first, two feet to the right, one foot to the left, with the flattened end facing outward from the first. Again I cast about, and soon I had found the third. It was placed opposite the second, such that the three now formed a triangle upon the top of the hill. All three were nearly filled with mud, and the first was cast out of shape by my leg having entered it, and so I could not discern the full width and depth of the things.

But it was curious. Very curious.

In the next two hours I sloughed my way to the other two hills in the triangle and made a thorough search. I must have looked a proper madman to any watcher, stamping about on the top of the muddy hills, sometimes dropping to all fours and taking to slapping the mud with my fists. But when I was done I was satisfied there was no more to be found in this place. Only the three half-moon holes at the top of the one hill. It was a curious thing. I could give it no meaning. And I must be getting back to Peyson to see about my young friend. To speak the full truth, I had no wish to be caught in the dark alone again, not until I was better prepared for an assault as had reached us yesterday. I still

felt weakened from it this day.

Cotton. Fool that I was, I ought to have come away with cotton to stuff in Kleof's and mine own ears. Tomorrow I wouldst not be so lax. The memory of the desolate scene we had ridden past this morn returned to my aching mind and I corrected myself. It would be this night that I rode forth again. Kleof and I would but wait out the darkness in the town, and take to the hunt again when the sun rose.

But how was I to take to the hunt? I knew naught where this beast might strike again, and had no track to follow, or known haunts to search. I racked my brain steadily as Kleof thundered willingly back toward town. But strive as I might I couldst not think of a plausible idea. Perhaps Turner might have learned something that wouldst help. Yes, I wouldst speak with my young friend. We thundered back to the town, and through the cobbled streets. But as we neared the inn, the noise bid me slow my mount.

It seemed Turner wouldst not be hard to find. As I approached the inn I was assaulted with the sounds of a mighty brawl. Shouts and yells, splintering wood, smashing glass, even the sharp smack and cracks of the blows could be heard. I allowed a sigh to slide from me as I dropped to the street. People were utter fools. And my irascible charge wouldst be inside somewhere. I packed Kleof toward the stable, drew my peacemaker[4], and shoved open the door. It rammed into the wall and the full weight of the sun behind me sprayed into the room.

"Cease thy foolishness!" I bellowed.

Twenty large loggers, the innkeeper, and four women locked in combat, stopped with chairs, fists, and glasses upraised. Every eye turned to me. My roving gaze caught a shock of red hair and I spied Turner. He was poised with a broken glass in his hand in front of a giant of a man who held a chair over my young friend. The glass fell from his hand and splintered. The noise of it filled the silence. I spoke again.

"Thou shalt return this room to order and walk out into the street. If thou must continue thy uncouth brawling, continue on past the end of town and do it in the mud of the wastes,

---

[4] Planistah has different uses for "peace" than we are used to seeing in our Western English. Often in the text it is used of things that help keep the peace; not things that are in themselves peaceful at all. This is such an example. A peacemaker is carried by many knights and most sheriffs upon Planistah. It consists of three hammers setup in a general triangle shape, which when struck correctly, all slam down with a combined force that can shatter any bone and punch through most walls. Around the hammers hang heavy chains that many have sharpened into spikes. I'll let you picture what those can do when they land a good hit. It is a devastating weapon.

where none shall be hurt but thyself in thy silliness." For another instant they stood, poised and staring at me. Then the man standing over Turner gave a snarl and heaved his chair. An aytem left my hand in the instant I saw his features churn with foolish, black hate. My weapon slammed bulb first into his head and the man went crashing over with his chair. As Turner scrambled desperately out of the way of the falling chair, my fist brought the peacemaker down on a broken tabletop. The thunder of the hammers striking the wood and splintering it in hundreds of pieces, eclipsed the sound of the man's fall. Chairs and glasses lowered.

"Out!" I bellowed, in no mood for the length of time it was taking them to comply. They scrambled to obey. Each combatant shuffled past me, eyeing the peacemaker swinging from my hand and the open aytem bag on my belt. My hand shot out as Turner filed past in the line. I gripped his shoulder, and jerked him toward me. The last shuffled out (one of the women, disheveled and with a tooth missing) and I slammed the heavy door. The innkeeper stood dazedly looking about him at the wreckage. I took the moment to propel Turner up the stairs toward my room, not bothering to

give a reason for it. If this man noticed us enough to be curious doubtless he wouldst put it down to my good-hearted determination to drive some sense into a lad. Knights were known to do such things. But my intention could hardly be called so peaceful, and my grip was a bit tighter than necessity warranted in my annoyance.

Chapter 8: Fists Fly! or Local Tensions

I was up and in the main room afore Arvi was stirring. 'Course he looked so out he may not stir till the afternoon dark set in, but still, I was out early. First I went to the kitchen and got breakfast. It were a pretty scanty thing, but at least it were something. More than I usually got in the old days, I told myself. But a lot less than I was used to at home now, my stomach reminded me as I grabbed the first of my deliveries and started to walk it on out to Ceedric. It were a box this time, heavy, but not as much as the potatoes. This one were headed to the barber shop. It was sealed, unfortunately, so's I couldn't peek to see what was in it. Something that didn't make noise when I shook it. I shoved my curiosity aside and opened the stable door to get Ceedric ready.

"Those are the stirrup feathers," I heard Ryam saying, somewhere in the midst of all the dust and dimness. "They breed those into merthyls to make them easier to ride."

"Can we ride him?" a young gal's voice breaks in, real excited. I stick my head over the stall and see Ryam sitting cross-legged there, with a shorter about two I guessed on his lap, a boy around seven maybe who looked real serious, and a gal of about five that Ryam were having a hard time keeping from dancing under the merthyls' paws as Ceedric and Kleof watched with interest. "Please, please, the little one, he is so pretty, can we ride him?"

"Let's get him out to the sunshine first," I said, and all four wheeled around to look at me. Ryam flushed, and quick stood up with the babe in his arms. He began to herd the other two out of the stall.

"I did not think you would be out this early," he said, almost annoyed. I grinned at him and whistled for Ceedric. Usually I would have fed him first, but he had eaten good not long ago and wouldn't mind one trip afore breakfast. I looked at the boy and flicked a finger at his little sister. "Think you can hold onto her good enough she don't squirm off him?" His solemn face lit like the sun coming up. He nodded real fast.

"You don't have to–" Ryam began, looking embarrassed, but I turned my grin to him and it shut him up. I shoved the door open and we all trooped out, Ceedric on our heels. It seemed real bright out here after the stable.

"What's your name?" I asks the gal, as she seemed like the talkative sort.

"Rawli. And my big brother is Reesom and the baby is Rachi and isn't he cute?" she demanded. I agreed he was cute, but she was off again almost afore I could, chattering about everything, until Ryam made her be quiet. I hid another grin and just got Ceedric to kneel. I motioned the boy Reesom on and he looked at me incredulously.

"I get to...alone?" he says, pretty soft and a little hesitant. Ryam's mouth fell open. Looks like it would be single rides instead of double. I pursed my lips like I really had to think about it as I studied the little fella.

"Think yourn man enough?" I asked. He lit up again, hitched his pants a little higher, and clambered up onto Ceedric. My merthyl hopped up and the boy gives a little squeal and throws his arms around Ceedric's neck. The merthyl grunted and froze, his nose flap going high as he looked at me. I laughed and showed Reesom how you pulled an ear to make him go, and how if you grabbed him round the throat he stopped. One reason Arvi'd picked Ceedric was because he actually liked shorters. Not just endured them, you know, but actually enjoyed them squealing and hanging off him. So the merthyl goes dancing around the inn yard, with the boy grinning and having a great old time thinking he's in charge. I sure ain't going to tell him Ceedric's going wherever he wants to, and keeping one eye on me to see if he is supposed to go somewhere else. After a few minutes I point the boy up the street and start walking toward the barber shop, the box thrown over my shoulder. Ceedric follows me of course, but I kept pointing out the way so's Reesom could feel like he were the one making the merthyl go that way, you know. It seemed to be working. Ryam fell in beside me, the gal on his back and the babe in his arms, as Rawli laughs and calls out advice to Reesom and pleads to be next. So's we get to the barber shop, I have Ceedric kneel again and leave Ryam to switching out the gal for the boy, and step in with the box.

There's only one guy in there. He's big like everyone else in this place, but not so beefy as most. His eyes go to the box and get real bright for an instant. Not like Reesom's lighting up though, this one was more like... a fever running through him. An unnatural light. He turns away next minute, like he wants to pretend he don't care. I don't show I noticed.

"Delivery from the inn. Mulk says you owe him forty-eight guilders for it," I says. The man don't balk, don't even answer. He just reaches into his cash drawer, pulls out the money, and switches it out for the box. But I seen that light in him again when he grabs hold of it. If this place had windows I'd sneak around to one and try to peek in to see what was in there when this guy opens it up. None of my other investigations have done anything, maybe this would at least tell us something. But there weren't no windows. I had to just turn around and leave. Chances were it were just otil seeds in that box anyway, with the strange way these folks were about vegetables. Still, forty-eight guilders...

When I stepped out of the place, it was to walk into a bunch of happy shrieks, and it made me grin. Rawli was on Ceedric and having a good old time all right, as Ryam leads the merthyl around and they all grin at her. When Ryam sees me come out he starts to lead the way back without no comment. Soon we's at the inn, and his siblings is off home, Reesom carting the babe, and both of them giving me and Ceedric a real big smile for thanks. It were enough. I led Ceedric into the barn to get his breakfast.

"Thank you." Ryam's voice was a little soft as it comes from behind me. I glance over my shoulder as I dust up Ceedric for the day.

"A little ride isn't much," I shrugged.

"To you maybe," he says with a smile. He hesitates a second then goes on. "Reesom used to say he was to be a merthyl breeder when he grew to a man. He hasn't spoken a word since Da died. Until this morning."

I nodded slow. I'd met folks like that, down in the dark ways where death stalked pretty regular. Mourning came in lots of different styles.

"Bring them on back and we'll see if we can make it happen again," I tell him, and he smiles real big at me. I head toward the inn to toss this money bag at Mulk. It's so heavy it's making my shoulder ache.

The morning moves along steady after that. Mulk has plenty of things for me to deliver and Ceedric and me are kept awful busy. All of it is little things this morning, no more of the giant bags of heavy vegetables or the sealed boxes. Somehow it made it seem less interesting. I was getting real bored with it when the sun reached the top of the sky, what my lesson books called "the zenith." When I come riding into the yard then I spy Ryam out emptying the ash again like when we first met, and I trot on over to complain.

"This morning it's all little things like letters saying folks ain't paid their bills, and I's getting real bored," I say without even a hello, and he looks amused. "Why were all the interesting things yesterday?"

"The cart came in yesterday," Ryam answered, and I stared at him.

"What cart?"

"The one that brings the vegetables to the inn, that Mulk sells. Mulk guards his sources well and won't tell anyone where it comes from. All we know is that it comes up the road from the south and is driven by a man with a face like a Ferret."

"No fooling? Has Mulk always had the same delivery man?"

"He wasn't making these deliveries when I went off to school." Ryam was staring at me now, looking curious.

"Tell me about this Ferret faced man. What's he like? Does he live around here?"

"No one knows where he comes from. He is a stranger, and as you know, people don't talk to strangers in Peyson, so how would they know anything about him? He might be a very nice man for all I know."

"You say that like you don't think it's true," I butted in fast. Ryam grimaced.

"My mother has always taught me not to talk bad about people behind their backs, especially if you don't know anything about them. Just because he grimaces and sneers all the time, and tends to kick at dogs if they get too close, and screams at children just to scare them, doesn't mean he's a bad person. He might have had a horrible childhood, like a brother mauled by a puppy or something."

"Mauled by a puppy?" I asked, pretty skeptical.

"It could happen," Ryam defended with dignity. I chuckled and changed the subject.

"I been meaning to ask, can you tell me about the folks what got killed by the beast? I mean the other folks, asides from yourn da."

"I suppose so... but I can't for long because I have to go clean floors before Mulk pulls out the rod." I opened my mouth to ask if he meant that rod in a metaphorical sense, then slammed it closed again. I probably didn't want to know the answer. He gives me the factlays, fast and sort of scanty, but enough I think, then ducked back into the inn where I hear Mulk yelling at him. I was pretty thoughtful as I trotted Ceedric toward the barn to give him a snack. And not just thinking about the wyrm mystery either. But I don't stay there too long. I'm curious about this cart, and I told Arvi I'd ask about the other folks what the leermackle-that-ain't ate. I might be able to learn more from the lunch folks. So's I head out across the yard, and around the alley to the back door. It's a dim mucky place, that alley, and I'm glad I don't have to lean in it long. The door's real thin and short, but I'm kind of thin myself. I slid on in easy, into the smoky dimness of the main room to a corner by the bar, where I can see things but not be seen easy. The stench of the alley switches to the smell of vol and hen meat roasting, good culloo, and even some chocolate pastries cooking. My stomach's suddenly growling awful. But I didn't bargain for lunch, just breakfast and dinner, so unless Arvi comes back and I can slip up to his rooms, I'll just have to tighten my belt for lunch. Could be worse. I could be having to serve tables hungry.

"Hi, merthyl boy!" Mulk's voice suddenly hits me, and I spin around. He's staring at me from behind the bar. So much for not being seen easy. "Head into the kitchen and gather a tray, the odd-jobber is too slow to handle all of our guests." I can't help a rueful smile as I do as I'm told. Tilmey's always had a superstition that if you say what might be worse, it'll happen. Some days it sure seems like he's right. But I don't mind too much because in a way this is what I wanted. An excuse to go out and mingle

with the guests and maybe get a few of them talking about that cart and the Ferret faced fellow. I want to know when he had showed up in town especially.

So I slid behind the bar, pushed open the swinging heavy door, and walked into the kitchen. The back door were open and it was brighter in here, almost cheery. Pots sizzled on the dirty stove, as an old hound dog watched them with hope shining in his deep brown eyes. He took a second to thump his tail on the ground in a greeting as he seen me come in. The cook was a thin old woman with a temper apt to leap up like a flame. We didn't take to each other. Mostly I think because, like a magnet, things that are real similar tend to repel each other. Maybe we saw too many faults we recognized too well, I don't know. Anyway, she scowled big when I walked in, and I scowled back at her, but we was interrupted by the assistant cook.

"Finally, another pair of hands!" he says, real relieved. I find a heavy tray shoved into my hands with two plates piled high with meat and potatoes. "Table five. Two out from the far wall, three in from the door," he adds as he realizes I don't know the numbers. I shove my back into the swinging door and push out into the dim

smokiness and buzz of talking of the main room again. The table I was sent to had two big old loggers and one lady what already had a teapot in front of her.

"Where is my scone?" she demands, real annoyed, as I get close. "I ordered it an age ago. You just get back ta tha kitchen and see what those lazy cooks are doing." She kept on as I sat the two plates on the table, and I don't got a chance to say a word and just have to go hopping into the kitchen again to see about her scone.

It went on like that for near an hour. Everyone wanted something, or was dissatisfied with what they did get. They were usually plain mean about the way they complained at it. Nobody would let me ask anything, and I were getting hungrier and angrier at every table. Finally, about an hour after I started, I were sent to a table with one big guy. A real big guy. He looks sort of slow, I notice, like maybe he's gotten too many knocks in the head, you know. But I notice it automatic because most of me was starting to sizzle. If Tilmey'd been there, this would be the time he'd be keeping his distance and getting ready to run for help when I blew it and got myself in something I couldn't get out of. Arvi would be quietly collaring me and shoving me in a corner to calm down, lecturing about self-control again. But, neither of them was around.

The guy looks up at me and something in his watery eyes seems to get a dim light, like he just had a thought. His big face changes slow into a scowl. His hand curved around his pint mug so tight the wood squeaked as it were smushed tight.

"You tha new errand runnah," he rumbles.

"Well, I sure ain't running errands now, am I?" I scowl. I plunk his bowl of stew down so's it sloshes onto the table. He stiffens and sits a little taller. The mug in his hand cracks and starts to dribble onto the table.

"I used to 'ave that job," he rumbles, slow and deep, and like he's getting angry. If I had been thinking at that point I woulda' walked away, fast, without saying nothing. But the hunger pushed my annoyance at everybody's meanness to real anger, and the red had already started to play with my mind. I stayed.

"You know anything about the cart what brings in the vegetables?" I asked, not bothering not to glower at him. "Where does the driver come from, and when'd he show up?"

"You took my job. I 'ad done tha errand running for ah year afore you showed up!" he

growls, the scowl cutting deep through his face so's he looks animal like. He's half out of his chair now. The mug is cracking worse and its insides is pouring out over the table and starting to drip on the floor.

"I ain't asking about yourn job," I says, feeling my face flushing and my shoulders squaring.

"It isn't mine no more. You took it!" Sudden he's on his feet and his fist is flying my way. I duck it pretty easy, he moves like his bulk makes me suspect, slow and strong. He stumbles forward when his fist don't meet with anything, and crashes into the table behind me, spilling the guy and gal there out of their chairs and splashing their food all over them. That guy staggers up with a roar and swings at my guy. My guy grabs him by the arm and heaves him over his shoulder, where he crashes into two more tables, messing up those folks' lunches. Well, then it all goes up in flames. Folks everywhere are grabbing other folks, swinging at them and throwing furniture and splintering glasses.

A big old logger slams on his back in front of me, as someone throws him. His hand shoots up toward my knee, as he howls with anger. I kick at his head, where Arvi says its softest, and he goes limp. But another guy tumbles over one of the tables, and lands on his feet in front of me, growling like a backthon. His fists come up and he starts swinging. I duck and land a kick on his kidney fast, and the guy doubles over, looking shocked. But his fist still manages to fly at me. I swing back, and hear that great old fist whistle as it goes past my ear, hear it even over all the roaring and yelling and crashing going on in this place. My hand flattens and slams into his chest in some of Arvi's methods. The guy folds up on top the other one, knocking a table over as he goes. Dishes fly from the table, covering the fighters around us with soup and tea. A broken glass rolls toward me and bumps into my foot. My angry guy comes running at me, the one what threw the first punch. His face is transfigured with real, real heavy anger. My blood's up and that red is running through me proper, and my hand scoops up the glass. I focus on this guy's kneecap as he runs at me with a chair swinging over his head.

Sunlight beamed into the room.

"Cease this foolishness!" Arvi's voice rings out over everything. Everybody freezes, and silence falls. My eyes fasten on the light. There he is, standing framed in the door, stiff and straight and perfect. Arvi's eyes are on me.

Sudden that red in me freezes into a sort of cold blue. My hand lets go of the glass. It shatters, and sounds like an explosion in the quiet. Arvi starts in again.

He takes over the situation and makes peace, like he somehow always manages to do, no matter how many people were ready to kill each other five minutes earlier. Folks listen to him. And it ain't just the way he holds a weapon either, there's something about his voice and stance that just makes folks snap to attention and do what he says when he orders it. So we all go headed out the door in a neat line, just like he says, when two minutes earlier we was trying to rip out each other's throats. He grabs hold of me as I shuffle past him, and he's beening certain. Soon he's shoving me up the stairs and into our room, and he looks proper mad this time. I stumbled over my big feet and near fell onto the wood floor. The door slammed behind Arvi and he spins on one heel. His other foot clonks into the ground with the force of it. He don't seem to notice as he stares at me.

"Thou wert prepared to lame him!" Arvi growls.

"He were about to spill my brains out everywhere!" I counters, feeling my face flush again.

"Thou can tell another's moods, sense things about them as no one else I have met. Thou knew he was not thine equal."

"So he was bigger'n me, that means he ought to be the one to stop—"

"That is not what I meant." Arvi's voice sounded plain cold, and it chilled my anger again. I do know what he means. Sudden I find it's hard to look at him, and my eyes drop. "Thou art clever-witted, Turner, and equipped with the skills and self-control necessary to turn and walk away. That man had not the necessary brain matter to be so responsible." I didn't say anything. I couldn't think of anything to say. A sigh comes from Arvi and he slumps just a little. He drops to sit on the bed, looking real tired. "What started the brawl?"

"Nothing," I mumbled. He gave me that look of his that says, 'That had better not be all yourn going to say,' and I listened to it. "He was the one what did the deliveries I've been doing for the past couple of days, and he was mad that he doesn't have the job anymore, and I didn't walk away when I should have. Then all the rude folks got mad at each other, and it went on from there. It had just started really when you came in."

"We were blessed I returned for the

afternoon," Arvi murmured, and ran a hand over his eyes. His headache must still be giving him trouble. "Thou recognizes thou ought to have walked away. But Turner, thou must learn to control thine own temper, I shall not always be there to save thee from it." He stopped sudden, his eyes darting away. Neither of us said anything. He ain't been there, not much this past year. After a few seconds I say something to get it moving again.

"I've been working on it." And I have. I had to. Especially after I near killed that bully out in Horner's Street, and his pals near killed me. If it had been any other guardsman on duty I would have been laid under the stone that day. But Kurtas Hornesly were there, and he actually watches, even the dark ways, and cares enough to help out, so he come barreling in to pluck me out. Kurtas didn't say much when he helped me to the doctor's house. That almost made it worse. But the doctor had a lot to say, and that made up for it. It took every trick of wheedling I had to keep him from going to Arv when my guardian came riding back in two weeks later. I changed the subject, pretty fast.

"Did you find the leermackle? You came back muddy enough," I says. Arvi looks down at himself and sudden realizes he's gotten the bed all full of mud. He grimaces and heads to the bath. I move to the bags to see if he's got anything clean left. He calls out from the bath what his day was like, and has me chuckling at the thought of him prancing around the hills stamping on the mud. Then I start to fill him in on my day, from Ryam and his siblings to the weird box, and then all the boring errands, and finding Ryam again.

"I didn't learn much about the folks what are dead now," I tell Arvi as he strips the bed of its muddy cover and drops to the sheets, toweling his hair dry. "But I did learn something. Maybe."

"What?" he asked as I stopped for dramatic effect. He sounds tired and annoyed. I decide not to draw it out.

"Everybody was to the south of town. Except the last gal, I'm not sure how she fits in, but all the others were out doing something to the south of Peyson in the mud wastes, and either didn't come back, or just the top bits of 'em were recovered."

"That is a fact to consider..." Arvi says, slowly considering it. He leans back against the wall, his legs tucking up next to his chest. "I wonder about the young lady. She does not seem to fit the pattern."

"Ryam didn't say nothing about her. He looked real upset for just a second when he hit the spot he should have talked about her, and broke off sudden to say he needed to go clean floors for Mulk afore the mean innkeeper pulled out the rod."

"Those were his words?" Arvi blinked. I could see him thinking about the lines speaking of widows and fatherless children, and had to work to keep the grin off. Arvi don't use his piles of money often, but as the regent of his family's estates (since his da was made ambassador), he's got more'n almost anyone else on Planistah. I knew he'd be using some on Ryam and his folks now, and it made me glad. Then his look sort of scrunched up, like it does when he's trying to think up a scheme.

"I shall travel out to the south road and see if there might be a place to watch for this ersatz leermackle. The difficulty will be doing so without becoming a target for the beast, whatever it might be. Perhaps I couldst dress Kleof and I in vol skins and mingle with a herd..." He saw me staring at him and broke it off.

"Vol skins," I just say. He grimaced and dropped his head against the wall again.

"What wouldst thou recommend," he says, a

little sarcastic, "does thy brilliant mind create a better suggestion?"

"Just about anything would be better than trying to dress up like a vol. I'm thinking the answer behind this whole thing is in that cart the Ferret faced one brings in. According to the angry guy what tried to crack my head open tonight, it's been around delivering stuff to Mulk for about a year, the same time the town started to spruce itself up, and about the same time Ryam's da disappeared. Maybe you should go tracking him instead of this fake leermackle."

"Thou just heard of it today, but a few hours hence, and know little of the matter," Arvi says, doubtful.

"But he comes up from the south," I butts in quick. "And there's something weird about these deliveries I's been making, it don't... something's just weird about them."

"'Weird,' what does thou mean?"

"I don't know," I say, my turn to be annoyed. "I can't give an answer I don't have. Something in my gut just says there's something wrong with it all. Nobody pays that much for vegetables without complaining, and purnaps shouldn't be that heavy."

"Heavy purnaps," Arvi says, flat. I dropped

onto the other bed with a sigh.

"All right, so maybe neither of us have much. But I think my lead is more promising than your scrabbling around in the mud. Why not come and work with me?"

"This morning I passed the farm where the young lady was slain." It's a sudden change in topic. But then I look again and know it ain't really. Arvi's eyes have that crinkled, tired look they get after some of our forays into the dark ways as Protectors. He's feeling heavy with the sorrow of the world. Like all that's wrong because of sin falls on his shoulders and he wants to fix it but knows he can't and it just makes him plain tired. I get like that too sometimes. It ain't always easy to leave the comfortable houses and go down into the muck and hurt. But it's always worth it to fix even just a little something that's been broken. Arvi, it makes him tired sometimes, certain. But it also makes him stubborn. It makes him cling to the work of fixing things like a bulldog to the nose of a bull. "The entire family stood before her stone, lamenting the death of sister and daughter, taken when so fair and young. I will not leave these people unguarded, Turner; despite their own pig-headedness which caused them to wait so long to summon a knight that six people now lie dead from this beast! I return to the mud wastes to see what might be found and perhaps keep the thing from overtaking anymore hapless souls. I couldst use thy sharp eyes, if thou wouldst patrol with me."

"In all that stinking mud? No thanks, I'll keep chasing down this cart and seeing what else I can find out. Say Arv, didn't you say that logger guy who told you about the dead gal said his son was interested in her?"

"Yes," he says, looking at me curiously.

"Did you meet the son?"

"No. The man's name was Ethlebight, if that is any help to thee."

"It might be, thanks."

"Dost thou still think lunch might be available after that brawl?"

"I don't know, but I'd better not go into the kitchen just now or I'm liable to take a swing at the cook," I admitted. Arvi stood up without a word and marched out. I could hear the stairs creaking as he went down to see what he could gather. Soon we was both tucking in proper, and were feeling better when we was done. Somehow having a full stomach makes life look a lot more hopeful.

Chapter 9: *Under Sparking Hooves* or *Second Encounter*

The sun slanted through the room's window when I awoke. I came nigh to cursing the headache which caused me to oversleep. It was almost the midst of the sunlit time of night! Turner was not in his bed, nor did the bedclothes look used. But the boy couldst take care of himself (I hoped) and I was late, so I did not search him out for an explanation. I must hie to the mud wastes if I was to learn anything this night.

Kleof was willing, if not enthused by the outing. We thundered out of Peyson toward the eastern road. I wouldst not proclaim our true direction in case Turner's theories proved correct and there were those in town connected with this ersatz leermackle. As soon as I knew us to be out of anyone's knowledge I turned Kleof from the well-packed clay of the road into the midst of the dripping mud wastes, to the southwest. The mud was not quite so wet today as it had been yesterday (it did not splatter up to Kleof's chest with each paw fall, but oozed and clung to everything it touched, such that he soon complained of the heaviness in each step). Above us the clouds leered again. Rain threatened to descend and make the place the freezing trap it had been when we were caught by the beast's scream.

The hills rose around us. The stench became such an inherent part of the ride we soon ceased to heed it. If one ignored the smell, the mud, and the bareness of everything, weaving in and out of the perfectly rounded hills reminded me of my home region. Of a sudden I found myself wondering how Father fared, as he managed the estate and served the king from a distance. He had not come to Hartsom since the first frantic days of regaining Charlie's throne and driving back the plague. I had found one occasion to visit Havingford, when out upon a mission for Servant Meagan. But though pleased enough to see me (I think) Father had soon bid me be back to my duty.

Kleof's deep thrumming growl broke through the still air as he gave an alert. I stopped him quickly, coming suddenly from my own thoughts and praising my merthyl for his good sense. I couldst hear it now that he brought my attention to the matter. Something moved just beyond our hill. The mud squelched and squeaked under the thing. For the sounds to reach us where we stood the entity must be large indeed. I slid a leg over my merthyl and

lowered myself slowly to the ground, to avoid making such noises as sounded from the other side of this hill. I took a moment to stroke Kleof's nose flap as a praise, slip a wad of cotton into each of his drooping ears, and motion him to wait where he stood. Then I began to creep up the hillside. It was steep and the mud slipped beneath my boots. But I was no stranger to these hills now and sidled up in a sideways fashion, moving in a z pattern. Thus I lessened the steepness and also the extent of the sliding effect. Soon I found myself nearing the crest. For a moment I hesitated then, but only a moment. I wouldst not be squeamish about it.

The ground oozed and squelched as I lay flat upon it. My belly seemed to sink into the red clay, such that it must be forming a cast of me. I began to shift upward, steadily and slowly. I used great caution as I eased my head over the top of the hill and gazed down to see what made such a stirring.

Below me on the flat ground between two sizable hills, a large framed vol moved on the fringes of a small herd. His coat was patchy, whole splotches of bare gray skin showed in the fading sunlight. I couldst count his rib bones even from here, for they stuck out nearly as much as his thin haunches. I slumped into the mud, greatly disappointed. Yet I did not stand. I stayed there on my hill watching the animals ruminate[5], and that one circle restively. Another joined the circling one after a moment. Three minutes later a third tossed its great head in the air and began to move, circling the herd in the opposite direction to the first two circlers.

They were growing restless as the sun went down. I too felt that restlessness. But mine was from a comprehension which these poor brutes couldst not have, for I knew the leermackle hunted in the dark. No, something else caused this stir. They smelt something in the air. Or perhaps they knew of something which had happened before, at about this time (a vol's memory is legendary). It couldst not be Kleof and I, for one had already begun the movement ere we came upon them. Something harried this herd. It couldst be only the smell of the coming storm... But my eye went to the sinking sun as the thought came to me. The beast I hunted came out when the darkness was upon the land. It was but moments till darkness fell. And it wouldst be a very dark night. I made my decision.

---

[5] Cows ruminate here on Earth, but it's slightly different with vols. They tend to stand in one place for a week or more, moving nothing but their jaws, when they ruminate.

I lay long upon that hill. The mud pressed into me and my klackmen felt heavy on my waist. As soon as darkness fell I slid cotton into my own ears, taking care to press it in well. I wouldst not be defenseless in the midst of that scream again. The moments ticked on. There are many difficult things about a soldier's life, but I have often thought one of the hardest is the waiting. Most soldierly duties are spent simply waiting. Tensed as a strung bow, unable to read or distract thy mind by any innocent activity, watching for the moment of supreme danger which thou hast been tasked to ward off. This was such a night.

I lay still in the cold, stinking mud as darkness closed over me. The hills in the distance faded into blackness. Then the hill across from mine began to dim, and even the vols below me disappeared into the dense blackness of a cloud-filled night. There was little to see. Darker shapes in the midst of the general darkness couldst be made out, if I strained. I removed one cotton wad from an ear. That aided my nerves, for I couldst hear the sounds of the vols then, and gauge their tautness, as well as listen for any untoward sound in these mud wastes. For an hour I lay thus. It was a weary watching. My head lolled upon mine muddied arm, as I let my thoughts stray to those I loved. To my stoic Father, the impish Turner, Charlie, Miss— I let my thoughts stray. My assumption was the scream of the beast wouldst forewarn me of its coming in easy time to prepare for it.

This night I was again reminded that assumptions were what slew most good warriors.

As I lay there I became slowly aware the herd below me grew more intensely troubled. Every one of the large beasts had left off their ruminating and circled about the others, some even moaning in their agitation. The stir of their great hooves sounded in a dense slogging noise, as the mud churned under their large bodies. I lifted my head carefully, beginning to pay attention once more.

Another noise invaded the night. It came to me as a thumping, as something hit the ground repeatedly, and then mingled with the soft creak of wood. As if a cart moved below. But its wheels must be square and abnormally thick to make such a sound...leastways they were not the rounded simplicity that made a cart roll smooth. Soon came another sound, of a merthyl moaning in its weariness, quietly begging for rest in the docile way of a servile cart merthyl.

The sounds swiftly drew closer to the agitated vol herd. The great animals circled each other at a quicker rhythm, and even in the dark I thought I saw their large heads tossing in fear. What might this be?

The creaks and thumpings stopped. The merthyl could still be heard, on the far side of the vol herd, almost directly opposite to me. But I could not see him. I could not see anything but darker shapes in the midst of the darkness. A shing of metal sang through the night. The vols began to low and the circling mounted to a faster pace. I slid slowly forward off the side of the hill, toward the strange noises. It was a risk. But I must see what this portended. And if I couldst see so little whoever drove that cart must be as blind as me. The mud squelched as I moved and I did not want such noise (though it was nigh impossible that it couldst be heard over the sounds of agitated vols below me). I lay flat again and allowed the mud to slide me down toward the chaos.

I neared the bottom of my hill, and the movement of the large vols was all that couldst be known to me. They were desperately churning at the mud, circling each other in the helpless, foolish manner of their kind. These vols might be thin, but I realized as I came to rest near the circling mass, they were not small. A hoof the size of a platter slammed into the mud two inches from my ear, and I jerked back just in time to miss the sharpened scallops upon the edge. A glance up showed a dense blackness in the outline of a frightened vol, far over the height of Kleof. Another walked behind him. The great head tossed and his three triangular horns looked very sharp against the darkened sky. I slipped and slithered to a crouch as the two middle legs of my vol passed me by. The back legs passed next, splattering red slime of the clay into my face. I dashed a muddied hand over my eyes to try and see again. The next vol was nigh upon me, for he had turned from the circle of the first and begun a new circle on the very outer fringes of his herd. I stood up with a bound, leaping for all I was for the three horns sprouting from the vol's forehead. My hand closed upon the center one. The vol gave a great heave of his head as he trumpeted his fright and displeasure. My arm was nearly jerked from its socket. But I held on, and found myself pulled into the air, clinging precariously to a vol as it spun to the right, into its fellows. It drew me into the midst of the herd of desperately circling animals. Their sharp hooves splattered mud all about me, as the horns tossed, and enormous

animal rammed into the next enormous animal.

This was not a safe mode of transport. Yet it served its purpose. As I scrambled onto my beast and lay prone upon his broad, bony back, I was able to take stock of our movements. The animal traveled steadily toward the opposite hill, where the sounds of the tired merthyl and strange cart had emanated. Perhaps I wouldst be able to see something in the blackness. Or I couldst leave my unwilling ride when we neared, and strive to gain a closer view.

A vol circling on our left rammed into mine and he stumbled to the right. I slid dangerously close to tumbling off the side, and lost my cotton in my desperate scrabble. Curse this mud! It made every surface, even the back of a bony vol, slimy and slippery with its stink. I calmed myself with difficulty and strove to gain a hold upon my animal's ear or horn. I could not reach either without sitting up and thus giving away my presence to any watching. My vol was circling again, his six massive feet slamming into the mud as he lowed and moaned and pushed his way toward the outer fringes once more.

A metal shing rang through the air. Every vol in the herd paused, as if it was the dreaded sound they had been waiting for. Then the circling began again, more frenzied (for such slow, methodical beasts) until it was traveling at almost a trot about the hills. I clung desperately to my vol, my head turned to try and see the area from which the sound came. It was not easy to spot, nor to guess its location. My vol was constantly being rammed by his fellows and I slipped and slid from one side to the other, ever in dire danger of falling beneath the sharp hooves of these panicked giants.

That shing sounded again, and yet again. The herd lowed and moaned, horns tossing frantically.

A shaft of lightning lit the sky above us for an instant. I lay dazzled, feeling as though my eyes were seared in the midst of their sockets. Yet in that flash I saw the vols in their gray with red mud splatters, a dim form of a cart and merthyl, and a mass of pulpy flesh between the merthyl and vols. For an instant I thought I saw a human form there, amidst the carnage of the slain beast... I could not be sure, the flash was so quick. Yet someone must drive the merthyl cart. It would not be a leermackle in charge of that. Thunder crackled and rolled over us and the vols (in their own fashion) went ballistic. Hooves tossed toward the sky as they kicked and butted against each other. Their trumpeting filled the night at such a level it woke my headache again, and drowned out all other sounds. My animal staggered as one of his fellows kicked him in the side. I had just time to jerk up and grab wildly for a horn ere his back hooves shot out, kicking his defiance against this night of terrors. My backbone snapped with each jolting kick as I clung there, my shoulder sockets taking the brunt of the force as I strove to hold on.

Another flash of lightning filled the night. I had just time to glance over my shoulder and saw the cart. It was moving. It traveled in an irregular fashion, rising high and then slumping low, ere it rose again. I saw just that much before the blackness closed again. I gritted my teeth and gathered my feet together under me. This cart might be naught but a poacher striving to gain the meat for his weekly sales. But something in me cried out that it was an integral part of the leermackle mystery. I must not lose it in the night.

Another vol traveled near to mine, slamming into him for an instant. My left hand closed upon the new vol's horn as my right hand loosed from my first ride, and I leapt. My boots skidded, but I managed to keep hold of the horn as the animal under me trumpeted his fear. I do not know if he even noticed me. Another rammed into this one, traveling the opposite direction. Again I closed my hand upon the horn and loosed the old horn. I was near too late in my losing, and jerked bodily off the old vol, so that I hung suspended from naught but a shaky hold upon one horn. A vast black shape came at me. A hoarse yell escaped me as I jerked myself up, my boots scrabbling to gain my animal's back ere I was caught between two ramming beasts and mashed to a muddied pulp. My left side and shoulder felt a massive weight as the vol slammed into mine. I was squeezed from between the two colliding vols with a pop, as of a buttered purnap from the grasp of a cook. I was gasping and groaning as I squirmed into a prone position on my vol's back but I was very alive, and even unbroken. There are some things to praise in the slipperiness of the slick mud, it seemed.

A quick swallow, a shake to clear my head, and I staggered to my feet again, grabbing for the horns. I played togglethrog over three more vols, then found myself upon the edge of the herd. Nothing but blackness and mud stood on my right. I let myself slide off. The fall jarred up my legs and I near slid in the wet clay (which would have been disastrous, as the middle legs

were already moving, they would have caught me full as I lay prone). But by God's good grace I staggered forward three steps ere I tumbled and rolled. My body thumped downward, into something shallow and rounded. As I came up again it was in a staggering run for Kleof, hoping and praying I couldst find him quickly in the darkness of this night.

The thing which I had rolled into was well known to me. It was the track of the ersatz leermackle. We were but minutes behind our strange foe.

Chapter 10: Bushwacked! or What Comes of Nosiness

I t wasn't until the third delivery that afternoon that something interesting happened. Arvi was still caved in our room, and I didn't think he'd be moving till the next morning. Though sometimes he set his own inner timer to wake up earlier than I expected. But that has nothing to do with the third delivery.

I come riding back to the inn, feeling bored and still a little annoyed, and Mulk hands me another stack of letters complaining at people what used credit and hadn't paid their bills. Well I hop back on Ceedric, spread out my map of town, and glance through the letters to get them in an order that would make them easiest to deliver. And there it was, two letters into the stack, "Erim Ethlebight" written in Mulk's scrawl. Looks like this afternoon might be a time to test out my theory about that gal. Or start to test it, anyway. I pulled Ceedric's ear and he thundered off, running up the street with his nose flap high and his ears wiggling at the fun of it all, convinced he was going real fast.

Even at Ceedric's pace it didn't take us long

to get to the farm marked out on the letter. It was a bigger one than most I's been to these past days, with tols and vols both, and a field of otil waving their dark green behind the house. And there right at the front of the place, training a real mean looking dog, was who I kinda hoped I would find here. It was the biggest of the three boys what had closed in on Ryam the day we first met. He glanced up when Ceedric and me came riding in. His round face took on such a scowl it scrunched up his mean eyes till they can't hardly be seen. Sudden I'm not sure how to ask what I want to know. What I tend to do when I'm still a little mad and want to know something, I go for the direct route, and hang the consequences. But I'd promised Arvi to watch myself. So I took another route while I thought about it. I dropped off my merthyl and hold out the letter.

"This is for your da, Mulk sent it over," I said. He squared up, staring down at me, and not taking the letter.

"What 'ave you and that blank Ryam come up with for me?" he says, that scowl trying to be a suspicious look and still stay a scowl. It made him look sick.

"It ain't for you, it's for your da. If'n you don't want to take it I'll carry it up to the house

for–"

"You move one step toward our 'ouse and I'll sick my dog on you!" he roared. The red was heating up in me again. I came within an inch of getting in his face and telling him to lose his old dog and I'd have Ceedric sit on him. But I'd promised Arvi. Instead I took a breath and tried again.

"Then you take it up. I've got to tell Mulk it was delivered, I can't just leave it here on the ground."

"Or what? You and that cheating Ryam will sick the beast after me?" His hand shot out, meaning to ram into my chest. I took a sharp step to the side. It rammed into air and he stumbled forward. The red was burning hot in me now. But I breathed steady, and shoved my hands in my tunic pocket, accidentally smushing the letter. I'd promised Arvi, and I'd keep that promise. But I gave up on coming at the thing delicate like, that's for sure. This guy would only understand delicate if a box of doilies hit him in the head.

"Are you mad at Ryam because you think your gal was going out with him, the one what got killed by the beast?" I said plain. His face loses its scowl and goes animal. Fury like a mad backthon takes over, and he lunges at me with all he's got. I dodge the roundhouse he has aimed at my teeth, but I can't quite dodge the left hook he has coming with the other hand. It connects like a merthyl kick on my jaw. I rocked, but I don't back off. Instead, as he comes at me with that animal fury roaring out of him, I let fly a kick at his ankles; and then I back off. He goes toppling over with a strangled grunt. My foot started automatic to sail toward his head, but I checked it, and stepped back farther. He grunted and growled as he started to shove himself up, but I didn't really listen.

Instead I reached out and petted his dog.

The critter's mouth lolled open in a happy pant and his tail thumped into the ground. I chuckled at the thought of him being loosed on Ceed and me. He might lick us to death. I slid the letter into his collar, hopped on Ceedric, and started off at a walk for town again. Ceedric wanted to run, but I wouldn't let him till we were out of sight. That guy was one what would say we ran no matter what we did, but at least Ceedric and me know better. And I can tell Arvi I kept his promise, I think, pretty pleased. I had really wanted to make that one kick an ocky, but I hadn't, and I didn't even yell back at him. We rounded a hill and I let Ceedric pick it up to a run and was grinning on my way into town.

I found three other boys about my age and a little older while I was delivering letters. I stayed on Ceedric when I asked each of them my question. They just knew it was because I don't have the guts to fight them. I knew it was because I didn't want to spread their guts around the cobbles and have to confess to Arvi that I did it. But even if most of the fellas in town thought me a low coward by the end of that day, it were worth it. I'd found out a thing or two about that gal what had gotten killed.

Every one of the boys fancied her, and seemed to think she was all theirs, and the other boys were thieving bovys what needed their heads stoved in.

I'd met gals like that. In fact, Layah's older sister Martah were one, always preening and cooing about the numbers of fellas she had strung out on a lead, and always going after more. Mrs. Trosk was constant trying to make her behave herself, but I'd been there an afternoon or two where Layah's ma were trying, and it sure ain't worked yet. The yells were almost as loud as some of the leermackle's screams. All right, so maybe not, but you get the idea. Anyway, this gal what got her head chopped off seemed like the same sort. Real pretty, but real ornery. Playing every fella she

could find and making herself look innocent and sweet while she did it. I ain't sure exactly how that helps us, but it gave us a better picture at least. With a life like that, I sure bet she had secret meetings with her boys all the time. Maybe one of them were out by the south road...

"Oy, watch your beastie there!" Ryam's voice cuts through my thoughts, as Ceedric side steps fast under me and I grab for his neck feathers to stay on. We was back at the inn yard, and nearly stepped on Ryam as he headed to the alley, lugging the kitchen garbage pail.

"Sorry," I mumbled. I'm sudden a little hesitant about the next part of my plan as Ryam smiles up at me. I were only thirteen, see, and I ain't got this hankering for gals that some of my pals seem to have concocted. Leastways, not the same, I just kind of looked on Layah a little different maybe. But I knew by now from watching them that it could hurt pretty bad if someone started messing around with it. Still, she weren't around no more... I dropped off Ceedric, sent him toward the stable to get some water, and fell in beside Ryam as he headed to dump the garbage in the alley bin.

"Ryam, don't get all fired mad at me, but I have another question for you," I started.

"You always have questions, and I haven't

gotten angry at you yet," he said easy.

"Truth yes, but not like this one," I say, letting a little of my hesitance slip out. He stopped dumping and turned to look at me, a frown starting to cross him as he studied me. I decide not to keep him waiting. He's been warned at least. "I know why those three fellas was so mad at you. It's 'cause Kaylar Bram chose to walk out with you, and the Ethelbight boy found out." His mouth dropped open for a minute, then slammed shut, closing into a hard line till I can't hardly tell he has any lips at all. "Look, I wouldn't be asking if I didn't think it were important, I would just keep it quiet and never say a word. But it might be real important. Do you know if she ever went out on the south of town, walking there with a beau or something?"

"I begin to think you are something of a heartless busybody," Ryam growls.

"I know, I know, but truth, it might be really important."

"Let me know when you are certain," he says, real sarcastic and pretty mad. He slams the pail into the bin to get the last bits out, and sweeps past me back toward the inn. I let him go. If he don't want to answer it, I weren't going to press it harder. Besides, by not answering, he kind of answered. I stand there in the mucky alley, considering his not-answer, and wondering if I should be concerned. Then sudden the shadows changed around me, flickering in different patterns. Someone was coming in at the top of the alley. I spun round and found Ryam there again. He still looked a little beening and he kept his distance.

"You are a heartless busybody–"

"I know, we's been over that," I start with a sigh, but he cuts me off.

"–but I think you really are striving to help your knight unearth this leermackle business. That cart you were interested in enough that you started a brawl such as the inn hasn't seen all year?"

"Well?" I prod when he stops, and have to grimace as I realize I sound like Arvi.

"It is here for another delivery, the Ferret faced fellow is inside at the moment waiting for someone to take his payment for the stores Mulk had for him."

I didn't pause to say thanks. I didn't pause for nothing, I just barreled out of that alley, in through the back door. It was near as dark and smoky in the inn as it was in the alley with the torches burning, and I took a second to stand and blink. But just a second, because I had a glimmer of what this might all be about, and this was probably my one chance to see about it. There's a thin, sharp faced fella at the bar, with the hard wrinkles around his face that show he's scowled and sneered his whole life. Probably even in his sleep. I slid behind the bar and head toward the cash drawer real easy, nodding to him like I knew he would be there, and scooping up a rag to polish a glass like I's always back here and it's second nature to me.

"How much?" I asked simple, cupping my wire in my hand. I's kept up my skill, using it to pick up a little extra spending money by unlocking things people didn't mean to lock; but mainly because it can come in real handy at unexpected times, like now. This lock is so flimsy it's hardly any lock at all. I open the drawer so quick and smooth it looked for all the truth like I's had the key cupped in my hands. I think it was that what made him shrug and assume Mulk had me back here to take care of it all. He steps a little closer, pulling out a big white bag, what clunked awful heavy on the bar. He tips it and a whole pile of tens come spilling out on the polished wood.

"Change it higher," he sneers. "And I'm paying this." He slides a dirty white scrap across to me and I glance at it to see Mulk's

handwriting, saying what he owes for the stores he's taking. So I change the ten pieces for forties and upward, taking out the difference for what he owes. Mulk's got a lot of high coins in his drawer. I may not be that great at the higher math, but I can do this at least. He's sliding his change back into the white bag and don't notice when I palm one of his coins and slide in one from my tunic pocket in its place. If someone comes to count, the right amount will be there, and I ain't taken nothing, or done anything shady, except pick open a lock. But I have something to look at now.

This Ferret faced fella slips his bag on his belt, swings his sack of stores over his shoulder, and stamps toward the door. I turn my back on him, like I don't care no more, and polish a glass, until I hear the door slam. Then I smack the glass and rag back on the counter and dust it out the back door again. I don't even notice the muck and smell or the smoking torch in that alley. My eyes are all on the gold coin I's fumbling out of my pocket. It's real bright, I notice as I hold it up to the torch light. There ain't no tarnish on it at all. Like it was new minted. I hold it a little closer to the torch, squinting at the inscriptions. The "t" in "tottlemeir" is off centered. I give a little grin, pull a five piece out of my pocket, and start to rub the copper over the gold[6] coin. At first it don't do nothing but squeal, and that's suspicious right there, because the gold should start to scratch, as it's the softer metal. But I use a little patience and keep scraping. After about two minutes I get what I want.

The gold starts to peel. Not just scratch, but peel. A darker shade is under it. There's just a coating of gold on this coin. I'm grinning like a fool as I flip it in the air and catch it again, and hear a chuckle slide from me. I's figured it out. That fake leermackle's just a cover for a counterfeiting organization. They needed meat to live on, and a way to get rid of those what saw too much, is my guess. A fake leermackle wandering the place would do it. Nobody would be looking for a poacher or murderer when you blame it on an animal. Animals just kill, they don't murder. Only people can do that.

I'm still grinning as I catch the fake coin and go to tuck it in my pocket. It's then I notice the shadows changing again. My heart sudden pounds and I go to spin round. But I don't make it even that far. A hard stick rams into the back

---

[6] All right, I confess it. I am guessing about the names of these metals. In all likelihood, they are metals entirely alien to Earth, and not copper and gold at all. But I knew you would understand those better, and my translations do make sense in the context.

of my skull and I feel myself crumpling toward the muck. My eyes go dim afore I land. But I still feel the splatter of the mud as it spurts up around me, and jerk up, automatic, trying to get out of it enough to breathe. The stick rams into my skull again. Everything goes black, and I don't notice the muck anymore.

Chapter 11: The Truth Looms Closer or More Tracking

I couldst see Kleof's ears in front of me. A dull gray light grew about us. It seemed to match the frozen cold. An especial clarity hung in the air with the cold, and I breathed it in with thankfulness. I was very glad to see something, anything, for it had been a black tracking. Slowly the hills around us turned to varying shades of gray. Then came the gold. First a sliver of it showed upon the horizon just to our right, caught in glimpses between the hills as we rode. Then the sky even above the hills began to lighten with the golden beams. Of a sudden the low-lying clouds became pink, seeming to shine with their own light. It melded into purple, then orange. Then all began to melt into the bright light of the newly risen sun, wherein all things took upon themselves their own color, and those colors seemed to be of greater luster than when last I was able to see them. You cannot see the color of the sun's light when it is once risen, but like a great and solemn truth, by it you see all else.

The tracks of the ersatz leermackle flowed on before us. During the night I had followed them sometimes by sight, when the moons had shown with enough light to see the black dents in the ground. Sometimes we followed by feel as Kleof's gate rose and fell through the midst of the tracks. It was a slow business, with much casting about from side to side, to be certain we had not lost the path, while ever striving to stay away from the shifting of the mud as it fell from the hills. Yet by God's good grace when the dawn's light found us, we were still on the track of this bestial cart. The oval indentions went on, ever overlapping each other, imprinted upon the soft clay. We rode another ten minutes as I allowed the sun to gain the height needed to see some distance. When the light about us had cleared the tips of the hills and shone down even into the valleys, I drew Kleof to a stop and dismounted. I was now accustomed to the peculiar way of these sliding hills and my heart was not so pained inside me. It did not take long to clamber to the top of the hill. But I did not mount upon it, for I had no wish to be seen for miles, a figure pasted against the sky staring out after the ersatz leermackle. I dropped to my knees and only my head crested the hill to gain a view of the area. It was enough.

The black trees of Jaspur fringed the land, seen most oft as a black smudge upon the horizon, shifting a little as a breeze caught the tips of the enormous conifers. Above the trees billows of clouds were gathering. It would not be long, I deemed, before another rainstorm came upon us. The mud wastes stretched out before me. Bare hills, a few with stubborn bits of half-dead grass waving, most with nothing but the red clay. Yet in the midst of the hills I couldst see what I had hoped and prayed to make out. The oval indentions of the ersatz leermackle could be seen for miles. It went deeper into the mud wastes, turning here and there as it wove between the hills, but going steadily to the southwest. I could not see the thing making the tracks, be it beast, or cart, or perhaps some monstrous collaboration of both. It was too far ahead to make out. Yet I recalled the glimpses last night and had little doubt of what I followed.

I turned and slipped and slithered back down the hill to Kleof. He was splattered with mud and hungry, but still full of heart and energy. I bid him move from the cautious crawl we had been employing to a steady canter. Mud spurted up around us as we pounded forward, but not as badly as it had in times past, for the sun had been given time to dry the ground at least somewhat. A glance up showed that was not likely to last. Clouds were swiftly rolling in to cover the sky. They blocked out the cheering light of the sun and appeared very ominous in their dark billows. Kleof cantered on. After a few minutes I bid him turn aside from the tracks we had been so faithfully following as a better way to the southwest opened beside us. For another hour the clouds darkened the sky, Kleof ran on, and I waited and watched. When the hour had sped under my merthyl's steady paws, I drew him to a stop again beside a vast hill, standing larger than its fellows by some ten feet. It took time to clamber up the slope, and when I reached the summit the day was darker still, as the clouds continued to gather and blacken. I heeded it not and merely pulled forth my eyeglass. This began as a standard issue guardsman spyglass. But Turner had made improvements upon it in the Trosk workshop. He had nearly ruined it thrice, but in the end it emerged better than before. With it I had a clear view for nigh on eighty miles, and couldst study things within that spectrum with a great clarity.

It did not take me long to spy out the track. I quickly followed it forward with my glass to my eye. It traveled steadily to the southwest, with only deviations to avoid the larger hills. But then the tracks deviated. They changed course with such a suddenness I couldst see where two of the tracks were smudged and off centered. It went due west for a time until – I started and nearly dropped my glass. The track had joined the cart. I couldst see it; a simple wooden cart resting one hill behind the main road through the mud wastes. Leastways I couldst see the top of the wooden cart and the poor drooping merthyl. The lower half was obscured by the hills. There was a single man at the front of the cart. The hood of a brown cloak draped over his face and the garment made him appear shapeless. The man sat up straighter upon the cart's bench and his cowled head turned toward the road, as though he heard what he had been awaiting. I spun my glass to the roadway. Another cart rumbled up the clay road. It was a very plain cart, pulled at a trot by two merthyls. There were a variety of sacks in the cart, all jumbled and shifting with each roll of the wheels. The driver of that cart was a very thin man. His back was toward me, and even through my eyeglass I could not have seen his face clearly for they were some distance ahead of me. But I couldst see it was turned to the side, as if he watched for someone.

As the two carts drew nigh the cloaked figure raised a hand, as though he hailed the other. The cart from the road turned in to the other.

Without any greeting that I couldst see through my glass, the merthyls were switched (the two from the road for the tired one we had followed through the dark), and both drivers began to transfer bags from one cart to the other. As they heaved up a long white bag, large enough it took both to lift it, the bag began to squirm. Only one shape that I was aware of couldst fit alive into such a bag.

A captive human squirmed within that white sack.

I snapped my glass closed, shoved off to slide down the mud to Kleof, vaulted aboard him, and was off. It would be a foolish thing to gallop in this slippery clay, and almost certain a way to end in a broken merthyl. Such would result in losing my quarry, especially with the rain eminent for it would wash away all tracks, and I knew not whither the cart wouldst go now that it had its new burdens. I would not let him reach a gallop. Nevertheless, Kleof surged off with a huff, his nose flap lifted high in determination, and we plunged madly into the mud. I kept him to the direction where last I had seen the cart, keeping an eye ever on the clouds. The mud churned under us, clinging to Kleof in red clumps and clogging his paws such that he appeared to be wearing thick boots. But my merthyl plunged on, ever faithful, catching my urgency. I noted even as he cantered he moved with sturdy caution, as if knowing a single spill wouldst mean disaster.

But we had only been traveling for some twenty minutes when the first of the fat icy raindrops tumbled from the clouds to splatter about us. I swiftly drew Kleof to a stop and mounted the nearest hill at a run, my glass in hand. It was a race against time now. And that squirming bag made the race of immense import. I reached the top and looked desperately for trace of our quarry. Rain drops splattered about me, already creating globs of the clay. But there, almost directly below me, the tracks of the ersatz leermackle traveled. It went on from there, and I quickly plied my glass to my eye running it along the tracks. It traveled in a southwesterly manner, then nigh a mile hence veered suddenly north. The rain was splashing more continuously now and beginning to interfere with long distance sight. I felt a shiver shake me as I ran my glass over the track, desperately striving to beat out the freezing rain.

The trail ended. I drew my glass away, blinked, and tried once more. I found the track again where I had left it, followed it quickly

north with my glass and then – Yes, it ended. There, in the midst of the mud wastes, with no sign of cart, merthyls, or baggage. I snapped my glass closed leapt off the side of my hill, and slid down, my boots making wet furrows in the softening clay. Kleof awaited me and sprang away as I leapt into the saddle, for he caught my excitement. I knew not what the sudden disappearance of cart and merthyls might portend, but I did recognize one thing as we rushed through the thickening freezing downpour. The end of our hunt was in sight. Our quarry had come to rest in their lair.

Chapter 12: In the Hands of Our Enemies or Awakening

It were real hard to breathe. Something was over my face, that's what was making it hard to get air in me. I went to move it, feeling slow and sluggish, my head swimming and sick. Something was moving and jolting me, on and on. Jolt and jerk, so's I rocked back and forth, and it don't help my head none. My arms couldn't move. They was stuck in something. I opened my eyes and saw nothing but white. My heart sped up and my legs started kicking without my realizing I told them to, as panic cut in. I shut my eyes tight, forced myself still, and just lay there, breathing as I could, and talking myself down. It's all right. God's still got me. I'm alive. And Arvi wouldn't be far behind. He never was. Not when I really needed him. I drew in another shaky breath and opened my eyes.

Everything was still just that white. But I could think a little now. There was something wrapped round my chest and stomach, locking my arms down. A belt maybe, it felt like it. The same type of thing was around my ankles. They was tight, but at least when I tried to move there weren't the real sharp pains that came when ropes cut through the skin, nor was there the deadness that came on when circulation was gone. These were just tight, not real cruel. Then there was the white what stretched over me. I lay still again, trying to make my pounding, sick brain work. It was material. A sack. I was in a white sack. And I as moving, almost certain tossed in a cart, from the way it jolted and jerked. All right. Now, what was I doing in here all trussed up? I closed my eyes again and slowly willed myself to remember.

The ferret faced guy. And the coin. Someone must have noticed me out in the alley. Fool! I cursed myself silently, furious that I hadn't thought to get full out of sight, like in Ceedric's stall or Arvi's room, afore I looked at that coin. It were too late now to get all fired up at myself for it. I had been seen, then I'd let myself be caught, and now I was just going to have to deal with it. I lay still again listening. There were creaks and groans if I listened hard, of moving wood. But it was all muffled through the sack what pressed over my face and there weren't much to hear. So I set myself to thinking instead, to keep my mind off the panic that kept trying to take over. I sure don't like this! Too many times I'd been helpless like this, and memories make the panic come on quicker and

harder, if I don't watch it.

So, counterfeiting. That's what this were all about. That's why the town was suddenly able to spiff itself up, and why everyone was so close and didn't want to talk to folks about it. Of course Arvi and Ryam both seem to think the folk's meanness was just because it's Jaspur, and they might be right. But maybe it was both. I guessed about the vegetables now, and why folks was willing to pay such prices for them. Mulk was the receiver, and the whole town was a money-laundering factory. These counterfeiters brought their stuff, once they made it, to Mulk. He paid them real gold for it, then divided out the dope stuff around town to different merchants and folks what dealt with quite a bit of money, getting it to them by way of the vegetables. There was probably only a top layer on most of those bags, and the rest was money sacks. The folks had to buy the fake money, but they would get more of it than the real stuff. So if you didn't count the fact that it was fake, they made a good profit off it. Mulk would count the fact it was fake. He was that type of miser, who'd want all the real gold and not the fake stuff. Which would make it hard to catch him out at the money laundering he were doing.

Which was kind of a funny thing for me to be thinking about, trussed up and caught myself, as I was. Arvi'd better be on my trail.

There was a sudden bigger lurch, what my head really complained at. A merthyl moaned out there somewhere. Then I think I hear voices. I can't be sure, but I think they's talking about me, the boy what was skinning a coin. Then somebody grabs my feet. I start squirming proper. There's no thought behind it, just instinct that says I ain't gonna be taken without a fight. Someone curses, the hands let go, and I drop hard back into the wooden cart. My head sparked and spun like Tilmey on a rope, and even the white went black for a second. Then someone grabs my feet again, and someone else grabs my shoulders, and I'm heaved over the side of the cart like the sack I am right now, with me squirming like a caught fish. The hands leave and for a second all I feel is air as I fall. I hit something squishy and soft and all I feel is sharp relief it ain't the floor of a wooden cart again. Then the smell hits. It's the wet iron of blood mixed with the sharp smell of a big old male vol. What air I do get I sudden find I'm wishing I didn't. I close my eyes again and try hard not to gag. Something bangs down next to me, then something that feels like maybe a sack of purnaps rams into my middle and settles, and something else slams onto my ankles and I lay there gasping. They really do think I'm no better than a sack.

A jerk comes and the purnaps jostle a little and settle in for the ride. Another jerk comes and we start moving. Whatever I'm in don't seem to move like a regular cart. It goes up, and up some more, and then it gets to the top of whatever it was going up, and rolls down real fast so it slams into the ground, and all of us things tossed in the back jump and jolt and shake with it. Then it starts to go up again, and the whole thing repeats. Again and again. Real soon I'm feeling sick, awful sick, and I've given up on thinking. Instead I's just praying and hoping the ride ends soon, before we has to go up and slam down again. But it keeps going up and down, over and over and over. My head is spinning so much I's not really properly there, when the rain started. It came down so hard it pounds even through the bag. And it just kept coming. Freezing water poured over me, and kept pouring. The cold were so sharp it woke me up proper. I really wished I were still out.

The rain stopped. Not slow, like how it stops normally, but all sudden, as if a cover's been drawn over me or something. I lay there shivering, my teeth banging into each other so hard that's about all I could hear, staring up at the nothing but white above me, gasping, and just dreading the next drop. The white turns gray, then black. I noticed that, but just hoped it were me going unconscious. But instead we go up again, and I shut my eyes tight, and then we slam and it's harder than before. Up, up, turn, and slam, over and over. We slam down again, jolting and jumping, and I ain't even got it in me to groan. But this time, instead of going up right off, we sort of rock, back and forth. Then everything goes still. I's so thankful I just lay there, and don't even think about where I might be now. I don't care, just so long as the going up and slamming down has stopped. Somebody grabs the purnaps off, and I's even more thankful. The bag leaves my ankles next. Then somebody grabs my hair through the bag. I's pulled up, tossed over someone's shoulder, and they start moving. I blink hard as I lay there folded over this guy, and force myself to start thinking again. After a few seconds of it I can focus on what I'm hearing. There are voices around me, and they're echoing. Like they's in a real big room, or something.

I'm swung off the guy and dropped on my bum. It jolts up my spine, but not enough to really snap my head, so's I don't mind so much. I sit there swaying, blinking in the bag and trying to decide if the light getting to me is a sunset or torchlight. It's orange that's all I know. It flickers a little, but that could just be my vision with the way my head is feeling.

"Let's see this coin skinner," someone says. It ain't ferret face, and it don't sound that angry. Something sharp sticks in the whiteness at the top of this bag. It pokes my skull, just a bit and I can hear the fabric ripping. Then the knife starts to slide down and I suck in air real happy like, as it comes flowing back to me. The top of the sack falls down and I can see. All I see at first is somebody standing right in front of me. A big pair of legs in brown pants that are grease-stained and splattered with mud, and a brown cloak swinging behind the legs. The knife keeps sliding down and soon the sack ain't nothing but a pile of dirty white, bloodstained rags that I'm sitting on. The guy steps back and I can take stock of where I am and what I have to face.

It's a cave. I ain't never been in a cave, but I've heard people talk about them, and even seen a few pictures in books. It's got rough rock walls that climb up and become a rough rock ceiling, pretty high over us. Though there's some sharp pink things hanging down, that at first I thought was some kind of strange light fixture, then I realized it was actually more rocks. Layah pulled out a book on caves once when we were at the library together, and was showing me all about the things what formed when water dripped down a cave ceiling. Stalactites I think they's called. Anyway, there's a lot of them up there. A whole lot. But I don't stare at them long because they're too high up to help me any, or hurt me neither. What's right in front of me is what I got to deal with.

Five people stand in this rock room with me. They's all the big logger types, where their heads nearly hit the top of these stalactites hanging down. Except one skinny one what looks like Ferret Face. He must come from a different region, because he is scrawny and sharp and not much taller than Arvi. This new Ferret Face leaned against the far wall, where I seen a dark hole what must have been the door out of this place. Two logger types stand in about the middle of the room, just staring at me, looking kind of just... there. Like nothing much interests them. Then there was the one with the knife. He ain't put the knife down, and ain't stepped away from me either. He's sort of leaning over me, ominous and looming. But right in front of me squats another guy. This one's black haired and real hairy, like a bush growing over his face. His eyes match his hair and they look almost as full of the spark of interest and life as his hair. Real dull those eyes. They's staring right into mine.

"I don't see why we couldn't have let our leermackle take care of him," Ferret Face grumbles. He's staring at me hungry-like. As if he wants to know what color blood I have.

"Because 'e might 'ave told someone else what 'e found out," the guy over me says. "Those othahs, who saw us airing tha coins from tha road, they didn't 'ave ah chance to tell anyone." The two share a ghastly grin over that one. Well. Now I know why those other murders happened. Not that it's likely to do me much good... The hairy one is still just sitting there, staring at me. Arvi, where are you!

"Speaking oof our leermackle, don't you 'ave something to do?" Hairy One says, still staring at me, though I can tell the words ain't to me. Ferret Face straightens up and leaves. No more words, no nothing. It sure is obvious who's in charge. Hairy One's attention is on me again. "Who do you work for, lad?" he asked. His voice was who spoke earlier, and it were just...there. Like he weren't angry, and weren't that interested. But not real uninterested neither.

Just there.

"I'm an orphan," I started, trying to buy time to think. I let my eyes open real wide, like I can't quite figure why I's here and what's going on. He waves it away.

"You probably are. But that has nothing to do with my question. Who do you work for?"

"Nobody, I chose to come out here," I answer, and it's true enough. I's working *with* Arvi, not for him.

"He 'as been asking questions all about town," the man with the knife growls. "About tha leermackle and Grackin and the vegetables Mulk delivers. Then came tha coin in tha alley."

"So you told me," the Hairy One says. He's just there, sitting on his heels, staring at me. The two behind him ain't moved neither. They look real similar, I notice sudden, maybe this Hairy One's the da of those two. Truth, they sure have staying still and staring figured well. "Chose or not, who do you work for? You would not be down 'ere asking questions for no reason, or on your own. You 'ave soomeone you are doing it for."

"I delivered the vegetables and I was curious," I said honest. But inside I'm wondering if this is the right story to be giving these folks. If they don't have anything to find out from me, then why would they let me stay alive? Unless... "The main point isn't why I found out, it's that I did. You fellas need a few more links in your system if yourn gonna keep this business up. Even the stupid guy you had delivering your greens would have guessed sometime. No one that can read a map is that stupid. But I already know. I can keep up deliveries for you and Mulk, and even help sniff out folks in other towns what might be interested in the dealership. I have an eye for finding folks like that." He was still just staring at me. But one corner of his mouth moved up just a little

"You are awfully obliging," Hairy One rumbles.

"Oh, not for free," I butt in quick. "I ain't obliging, not at all. I'm ambitious. Just a little, see, I don't want much. But if I could get a small pile laid up, I could go where I want and maybe set myself up in some business or another. Like crackjacking."

"Crackjacking?" the guy asks, for once showing a little emotion, like he's thinking it's a real surprise someone as young as me knows about that. Then he kind of snaps out of it and goes back to looking real even. "I don't believe you. Who do you work for?"

"I told you–" The guy's knife handle rams into my cheek. I sag to the right helplessly, and smash flat on the rock, desperate trying to keep my sparking head from bouncing.

"Who do you work for?" the guy in front of me asks again, in the same even voice. I hear it, but I can't see him just then because everything is spinning. The pain is so sharp it pounds in my eyes, and all I can see is white sparks. It starts to clear quick. The sons ain't moved at all.

"No one," I grunt, and it's hard to hear from the buzzing going on in my mind as I lay there all stiff on the rock. Knife Guy steps a little closer. But Hairy One glanced at him, and Knife Guy steps back again, glaring at me. The kneeling one, what is sure in charge, swiveled a little to face me in my new position. His face hadn't changed at all. It still just looked business-like. Almost bored.

"Amon could get an answer out oof you. He is very good with that knife oof 'is, and 'as many surprising uses for it. But I 'ave nevah 'ad much faith in those methods, answers pulled from ah person are often tha wrong answers in tha end. But, I will ask you one more time before we kill you, and tell you now; if you answer me, truthfully and willingly, it will be a swift easy death. Just a beheading from our little leermackle." The guy showed the first expression yet, his face softened a little and he smiled, like he was speaking of his favorite hound or something. Then he snapped back to me and went back to plain with no expression. "If you choose not to answer, I'll let Amon kill you. That would be neithah quick, nor easy. I will ask you one more time–"

"Wait, wait," I break in, trying desperate to think of an angle and stall a little. "Why are you so certain I's working for someone? I'm a busybody, just ask Ryam at the inn–"

"He is no good to us. Ryam is no good to anyone aftah tonight," Knife Guy growls, and I go on fast.

"All right, ask anyone else who's met me, I just go poking my nose in things that ain't my business, all the time. I don't have to work for someone to do that!"

"Your questions were too specific for simple curiosity," Hairy One states. "You 'ave been trying ta find out about us. Who set you ta it?"

"Sure I's been trying to find out about you, I guessed what it was about and wanted in on it!" I blurt out. Amon's boot rams into my stomach so hard I slide a foot across the rock floor. I curl up with what would have been a groan, but I don't got the breath for even that, and just lay

there fighting to breathe again through the ache.

"Answer the question," Amon growls. If I answer the question one way or another I's gonna be dead. I have to try and stall, so Arvi can find me. But as Amon steps closer and even Hairy One frowns at me, I know that's not going to hold. Then it comes down to how... If it were just me, I'd tell them I was working for someone, maybe make up a name so's Arvi ain't in more danger than he already is, and go for the quick way. While I would rather not be dead just yet, I know I'm covered by the Savior's blood; death I only fear so much. But real long, painful death from real nasty people... Now that scares me proper. I know just enough to understand what it means. If it were just me, I'd pick the quick way and just keep trying to talk my way out of it until the end. But it ain't just me. Arvi will be here soon. He always is when I really need him.

Isn't he?

This past year parades through my mind. Sudden my heart's shaking, as fear turns to throat-swelling, sweat-soaking terror. I ain't so sure. He hasn't always been there for me this year, even when I really desperate needed him. Amon leans over, his knife flickering in the torch light as he turns it this way and that. I can taste iron in my fear. Pains from the past roar through me and fire pulses under the scar tissue on my cheek. But it is scar tissue now. Arvi did come, that time. And other times, lots of others. He's more'n just my guardian. He's my brother. He will come. He's got to come. Won't he? Hairy One shifts a little, about to ask one more time. I know it'll be the last time. I got to make a decision now.

"Who are you working for?" Hairy One asks again. I set my teeth and don't say a word. Hairy One waits for a few seconds. Then he stands up smooth, turns around, and he and his sons walk out without even a glance back. Amon looks down at me and a smile goes over his face, a look that's real worrisome. He flicks his knife blade in the air, letting it catch the red torchlight so's the blade is sparkling red, then catches it again with a laugh. It's a real evil sound, that laugh, and I find I's in a cold sweat as I lay there.

I've bet everything on Arvi. I chose to give him a little more time to get to me before I'm dead. If he doesn't come soon... I swallow and force myself to breathe again. Amon grabs my hair and jerks me to a sitting position and I let my eyes close.

Arvi had just better come soon.

Chapter 13: In the Leermackle's Lair or Hunt's End

I watched Kleof carefully as we neared the end of the ersatz leermackle tracks. If my merthyl caught any scent of people near, he wouldst alert me. Of course, we still threaded our way through these mud hills with their sharp smell, even his senses may not be able to overcome such a stench. We rode dangerously close to the hills, mud oozing down in patches or even tumbling off in great heaps in some places (we were near buried twice). But I would ride close to keep us from immediate sight of any watchers. Lord willing, we wouldst remain hidden behind the hills. It depended much on where the cart disappeared to, and if it was deemed necessary to have a watcher upon the hilltops. We rode on, beside the shifting hills, the muck striking up at us with each paw fall, and both of us shivering, soaked by the rain. The downfall had not lasted long, but it had been a hard storm.

A movement caught my roving eye. My hand shot out and closed over Kleof's throat, drawing him to a stop as I stared at the place. It was three hills forward, at the summit of one somewhat greater than its fellows. Something had moved thereon, I swore it. Five long minutes ticked past as I stared at the place. Then it came again, that small movement. This time I couldst see what it was. A head appeared over the crest. A guard detailed to watch each direction, but keeping it as stealthy as possible. We stayed perfectly still, unmoving in the shadow of our hill. We could hear the plop of mud as it oozed and fell from the hills to settle upon the ground and begin the formation of new hills. The head ducked behind its hill again, studying the land from a new direction. I urged Kleof forward, whispering in his ear for him to move swiftly but with as much silence as possible. We darted forward, the mud still slucking and pulling at us, and my gaze never leaving the place wherein the head had appeared. At least this head was still attached and alive, unlike the ersatz leermackle's victims. I cupped an aytem in my palm, never taking my eyes from where the man had shown himself.

Black hair appeared at the top of the hill, as he began to turn back to our direction. My hand lifted and the aytem flew upon its errand. It was a long shot but I had made longer. The man's face rose to full view and I saw him start as his gaze caught Kleof rushing toward him. My aytem's bulb caught him full upon the forehead. The figure toppled backward, out of our sight, and I bid Kleof run. We must arrive before the alert rose from another quarter, perhaps a second watcher, a camp upon the far side, or someone who heard the thump of the fallen man.

As we neared the hill and I drew Kleof to a stop, I couldst hear nothing but the settling mud. I leapt down, dropped to my belly, and eased my head around the corner. Nothing but more hills. I shuffled yet farther. I saw the fallen man, seeming more a lump of clay than a man after he had rolled down the hill. As I stood, my boots squelched and threatened to slip upon the slimy clay. I mastered my stance and began to move toward the fallen foe at the bottom of this hill. My eyes roamed ceaselessly, and one hand rested in my aytem bag. But nothing moved. Nothing seemed out of the ordinary. Kleof gave a huff, asking if all was well. I let out a low whistle, telling him he couldst approach, and walked slowly forward. The hill seemed as every barren mud hill we had come across thus far. If only the rain had not washed the tracks of the cart away!

I could see nothing out of the ordinary. All was red clay, squishing under my heel, rising into the vast hill, sliding and oozing– Wait. There was one odd thing. In one section of hill above me the mud did not ooze or re-settle as was the wont of the rest of these lands. It stayed smooth. I quickly moved toward the spot to get a better view of the anomaly. The patch was perfectly circular. The hill under me slid down with each step, as though trying to form a new hill and make me the center of it. But I wouldst not let that deter me and scrambled up, striving to reach the circle. A bony muzzle landed upon my rump and shoved, and I found myself propelled up toward the area. I shot a hand out in shock and it slammed into the bottom of the anomaly. The entire circle (its radius as tall as myself) shifted under my blow. I landed upon the mud of the hill with a wet slap and slid helplessly down. I found myself thumping against Kleof's great front paws. His head lowered and he nibbled my hair. A low moan came from him, as if to say "Why did thou come back down when I helped thee up already?" I gripped his neck and used it to heave myself to my feet again.

"Come, good fellow," I murmured to him, placing a foot upon his muzzle. "Grant me thine aid again." He shoved me violently upward. This time I twisted in midair and managed to slam my filthy boots into the bottom of the circle. It flipped. I sailed through it, into a darkness that left me blinking and momentarily blinded. Blackness and a man cursing in shock surrounded me. I slammed onto something hard. My boots slipped from the mud encasing them. I landed flat upon my back. Something metal whistled over my head, and through the white dots blinking in my half-blinded eyes I spied a silver blade cutting clumsily where I wouldst have been but for the mud. A throwing dagger whipped into my hand as I lay prone, and out again, toward where the wielder of that blade wouldst have to stand from the angle of his blow. I heard the gasp and gurgle of its landing, as I flipped and crouched, Peace leaping into my hand. A thin, pinched man was on his knees, one hand fumbling for my dagger. It protruded from his lower right side, his eyes frantic and confused as if he strove to grasp what had just happened.

I leapt toward him to bring the man to unconsciousness before he couldst gain his wits enough to call for aid. My boots shot out from under me with a wet slucking sound. My hand came up with an aytem and flung to deal with the enemy as I flailed in midair. Then the hard rock of the ground smashed into my backbone again, and I heard the wind of the air leaving my lungs. I lay there, gasping, and staring up at what appeared to be the ceiling of a rocky cave. The mud where I had entered was an ingenuously crafted wooden frame, doubtless with clay baked upon the outer side. So much I saw as I lay gasping for breath again. I sat up with a groan, my spine popping in complaint. Some days it seemed I was not as malleable as I had been at eighteen. My head swiveled quickly as I began to jerk off the slimy, offensive boots, taking stock of the room and what I might have to deal with.

It was a rounded cave. The sacks and boxes stacked about made its use as a storeroom obvious. Two merthyls were also stored here, in one corner of the place. The beasts stared at me from a miniscule pen, their patient triangular eyes looking hopefully from me to the bin wherein their food was kept. It seemed they were not concerned with alerting their masters of an intruder. Beside the small pen was a curiously empty storage area. It rested between the pen and where the boxes began to stack and it took the form of a square. But upon the rocky floor of that square two indentions had been hewn, by obvious human workmanship. They were the same cylinders, slightly overlapping each other, which I had been following these past days.

My ersatz leermackle lived here when not out rampaging. I had found the lair of this beast which had plagued this land. Well, I had found a portion of it. I dropped my muddied boots upon the cave floor, and began to march toward the black maw of the tunnel leading out of this storeroom, deeper into the lair of the beast, my stockinged feet silent as I went. Peace glinted naked in my hand. I wouldst find out more of the monsters living in this den.

Chapter 14: The Knife Blade and The Dead Body or Discoveries

A mon kept a hand on my hair, and stuck one leg behind my back, so's he could bend my neck over his knee and have a better view of my face. It weren't exactly a situation I liked. My brain was working furiously as he shifted his knife around and around in his hand, studying me like an artist trying to decide where to start on a painting. Maybe I could at least distract him!

"Ryam, you knew him," I said. It came out in more of a squeak than I meant it to. The guy looked at me. Almost curious. "I was just wondering if you knew what happened to his da. You wouldn't happen to be the one what killed him off, would you?" A real nasty leer goes over the guy's face.

"We payed 'im to excavate these 'ideaways," Amon says. Limeny, almost like he was a bad guy in a book, you know, where the hero wants to know something and just like that the bad guy starts talking. But then I guess it really is in human nature to tell what we's been up to. We all like a good boast now and then. This Amon gives a bark of laughter. "Not in real money, oof course, but 'e didn't know that. He was ah good minah, and ah 'ard workah. But we couldn't let 'im 'ead ooff ta tell people what was 'ere. It was Tully who did it, set up 'is vol blade so it slid in on tha minah when 'e opened tha door ta 'is beloved room. Chopped 'is 'ead ooff with one quick slice. It was aftah that we thought oof tha leermackle. Especially aftah that greengrocer looked right at us as we aired tha coins one night, and we 'ad ta do something with 'im. But that isn't why we know about Ryam tha odd-job boy, 'e 'as earned it all for 'imself. Now, tha only sound I want ta 'ear from you is ah good scream. Maybe tha tongue should go first..."

He started to stare again, poking at me. I went back to banging my brains around, looking for a way out. It weren't doing me no good. I was trussed up firm and couldn't think of any way to get out of this mess. Instead I switched to praying frantically, begging God to get Arvi off his stupid track-following and tag after Ferret Face like I told him, at least long enough to find me! Amon's face screwed tight and the tip of his tongue stuck out the side of his mouth. He brought his knife toward my scarred cheek. The blade was cold as it touched me, just under my eye, and I felt myself twitch despite all the courage I could dredge up. Sweat dripped down my spine. Amon grinned and the

knife pressed harder, but not too hard yet. He was relishing seeing me cringe.

A shout comes from the room behind us. Then something crashes, and the shout turns to a scream. Amon spins around and he don't even notice the way my breath blows out, my whole body shuddering in relief. Two battle cries rise over the scream, and another crash comes. The scream goes silent. Amon curses and makes a run for the tunnel out, shoving me away so I slam back on the rock again. My head goes bouncing and, truth, do the sparks fly in my mind. But I don't bother with it so much this time because it means that Amon is gone. The battle cries die in a sort of strangled grunt. Amon's reached the tunnel entrance, his knife flashing and his face murderous.

A silver star comes slashing out of the black tunnel and rams smack into Amon's head. He don't stagger, he just goes back, flat as a board. I feel the floor shake as he lands. But I ain't really paying attention to that, because I know the silver bulb skittering across the floor. I can feel my cheeks stretch at the grin what goes over me.

Arvi strides in. His holey stockings are slapping the floor and Peace is out in one hand, and I's hardly ever been so relieved and pleased to see him. I can feel my eyes dancing, that's how happy I was when I saw him walk in like that, all muddied and bloodied in his stocking feet.

It's all right. Everything's still all right. He came for me.

"You complain about my smushed hats, but you never took the time to buy yourself new socks," I commented.

"No one sees my socks," he says, not at all surprised to see me there. He drops down on one knee and his hand runs over my scalp, probing my wound. It stings a little. But I don't mind his hand on my head. It ain't like that Amon. "Thou does not seem in very evil straits."

"Yet," I adds as he goes to unhooking the belts wrapped around me. I find I's grinning, and that relief has stayed and bubbled on till I feel almost giddy with the warmth of it. Arvi came. Just in time, and just like I knew he would. Everything's all right still! But I don't say none of that to him of course. What does come out is, "Thanks."

"Art thou able to move thyself?" he says simple.

"Truth yes," I answer, feeling like I could have flown if someone asked me just then. I stagger up, teetering a little as my muscles get

used to being able to move and having the blood come to them right again, and smile at my pal. "I know what it's all about!"

"Counterfeiting."

"Aw, Arv! How'd *you* find out?" I ask. He shoves a thumb over his shoulder at the tunnel, and I follow him on through, pretty disappointed that I couldn't spring it on him. It's another cave room, bigger'n the last one, with these white rock formations on the far wall what look like pretty crystals gathered into tubes, all in a line from ceiling to floor. It was like snowflakes made bigger, none of them quite the same, and all of them real delicate and pretty. But there's more in this room than just the cave formations. All the goods are in here, from the molds and smashers, to the gold smelter and copper kettle. There's also Hairy One and his two sons, fast out, with great old bulges on their heads from where Arvi's aytem bulbs have rammed into them. One's also bleeding all over the floor from a hole in his thigh, but Arvi's already ripping the guy's shirt to bind up the wound and stop the bleeding. I go to pick up a mold, studying it. They's real good. The only thing wrong is that off-centered t, and it's barely off.

"I wonder if they has a pile of coins ready to

be aired around here somewheres. I bet they do," I says, starting to rummage around in the piles of junk.

"'Aired?'"

"It's the term for when you make the money and it's fresh off the molds and presses and you take it out into the sun. You have to lay it out in the sun for several hours so the soft top metal can proper stick to whatever cheap base you picked. Otherwise it might start to peel when you hand it over to whoever it is that switches it out for the real stuff for you. There's always someone who buys the fakes with real money. This time it's Mulk at the inn."

"Oh. I wouldst like to find that, but I am more interested in finding if they have a pile of real coins here. That might be related back to those who paid it. Let us explore farther." Arvi heads toward the only other door in here, a thick, simple wooden thing. I fall in quick beside him. He grabs hold of the latch and pulls, but it sticks. Arvi grabs his wire from his pocket and starts to twist it right, but I's too preoccupied to even be proud of my student, as a thought's occurred to me.

"Hey Arvi? What do you think they's done with the rest of their victims? I mean the bodies that don't have heads anymore," I clarified,

staring nervously at the door. "They would have to put them somewhere to keep folks from knowing it didn't get eaten—"

"These mud hills wouldst cover anything and keep it hidden." He pauses in plying his wire to grab a torch from a pile and light it at the one hanging off the wall. I grab one too as Arv goes back to the door. "Perhaps the answer will come during their trials, but if I were one of these monstrous villains the bodies wouldst have been shoved into a hill in the midst of a rainstorm." The door came open with a crack, like it hadn't been used in a while. Something brown was caked round the edges and stained the ground. And a smell wafts out.

"Unless I had murdered a man outside the mud wastes," Arvi comments. I glance past him and gag, pulling back. "He is almost skeletonized, do not react so. Let us see what was worth being murdered for in this cavern." Arvi steps over it and heads into the darkness, his torch flaring high as it eats up cobwebs in there. I look up at the ceiling and follow him, scurrying along at the sides and holding my breath so's I don't have to smell it. I'm past after a minute, and run to catch up to Arvi. He's striding on, and doesn't even seem to have looked back to see if I was coming. This is a tunnel, narrower and tighter than the others I's glimpsed in this place, with just simple gray rocks. Even the spider webs die out as we go, and there ain't no life but us down here that I can see. I'm guessing, from that thing at the top, that we's headed to Ryam's da's "favorite room" as Amon called it. But knowing that doesn't help much with the dark and close. After about ten minutes of it, I decide I can't stand the silence no more.

"Limeny, Arv, it's still going down." My voice echoes, sailing out in front of us and then bouncing back again.

"There are no divergences in this tunnel," Arvi answers, real steady. But I notice he keeps his voice quiet, almost whispered, so's not to wake the creepy echo. "Even if our torches burnt out we couldst still return from whence we came."

"Fine, but I'd rather not let them burn out, if you don't mind. I's been under the city plenty of times, but never under this far, and to be dark too–" Arvi stopped short in front of me and I face-planted into his back.

"Turner?" he asks, real quiet. I get a shiver up my spine at the way his voice sounds. "Dost thou see a light ahead of us?" I took a deep breath to steady myself, then leaned around my

pal. There was a glow coming up to us, from somewhere ahead. It were real faint, but it were sure there. A real unnatural glow. I swallowed hard.

"What if all those bodies was dumped down here, and now it's a haunted cave!" I hear myself squeak. Arvi's hand slams into my shoulder and I trip over my foot and go bashing into the cave wall.

"Do not be a noodle-pate. God kills and makes alive, there is no in-between of ghosts and ghouls. Come, let us see what is creating that light." He strides on again. But I notice he has his hand on Peace as he walks. I run pretty fast to catch up to him. I don't want to be left alone for a minute in this place. With every step that glow gets brighter and closer. Soon its shining on our feet and we can see by it better than by the torches. I blink as I walk, and notice something. This ain't just a single glow, it's a bunch of little ones. There's orange and blue, red, white, yellow, purple even, so many colors all mixing and dancing together. Arvi slows down and I look up at him again. He's at the lip of a kind of entryway, a hole where the tunnel dead-ends, and the light shining all around him. His shoulders square and he steps through, his hand still on Peace. I bite my lip

and follow on his heels.

Those lights sparkle all over me. I see more colors now, some I can't even name. I lift my eyes, kind of slow, not sure what I'm going to see. I can feel my mouth dropping open and my eyes drying out they're so wide.

We're in an enormous cavern. It must be as big as Charlie's Judgment Hall, or even bigger! Hanging down from the ceiling are stalactites, I guess, but they's like nothing I's ever seen. Have you ever dissolved sugar in water, then set it out with a piece of wood, and watched what grows? They look a lot like that, great old crystals hanging down, all snow white. Some of them are so long they come down to a normal ceiling height over my head, and I can see them clearer. They're sparkling with the reflections of the lights, sending out the colors so they bounce and dance everywhere. I tear my eyes from the crystal ceiling and my mouth drops open farther. The walls of this place are filled with jewels...I guess. Maybe? If they are jewels, they're living ones. Whatever they are, they are all perfect ovals and squares, dotting the walls all over the place, or clustering together in fantastic piles on the floor. All of them are glowing. It seems to be with a light of their own, just glowing and shimmering and all of them

seem to have their own color. A drop lands on my nose and I pull back a little, staring up again.

"Something's dripping off the ceiling," I mutter, too awed to say anything else. Arvi takes two steps in, slow, his head turning this way and that. He looks dreamy, and real blowed. His hand goes out and he catches a drop on his finger. He sniffs it, then touches it to his tongue.

"It is dark. And somewhat bitter. Like unto iron perhaps?" he murmurs.

"Why iron? Have you really been developing an analyst set in your taste buds?"

"Curb thy cheek, I said perhaps iron. Hast thou not heard of the Niathalins's glowing rocks? I wonder me if this was their source, where the rocks originated."

We don't say much more. We just stroll through the place, awed by the beauty of it all. Each new curve brings a new wonder. There's glowing triangles, and pillars of shining black, and fantastic rocky shapes winding round each other like wyrms and...it's too much to tell you about here. It's too much to tell anyone about. But finally, as we's walking, my mind starts to go back to what we left up there in the rest of this place, and that makes me think of the thing we had to step over, what made it possible to get into this place, and from there I start thinking about Ryam. And that starts to get a cold prickle down my spine again.

"Hey Arvi?" I ask, starting to get that creepy feeling of something wrong.

"What, boy?"

"Did you find a thin, ferret faced fella' back there?"

"No."

"What about a sharp blade, whatever it is they's been using to chop up folks? Or the cart, was that over there at the front?"

"'They have,' Turner, thine grammar has slipped abominably since I have been away. Nay, I have seen none of those. There was a place for the ersatz leermackle (most certainly this cart thou speaks of) but it was not there when I entered. Why dost thou ask?"

"I think they're out after another victim. They knew about Ryam."

Chapter 15: Ryam's Part

My shoulders smarted from a new bruise as I walked home that evening. My thoughts were almost as black as the clouded afternoon sky. Mulk had only gotten one blow in before I ducked out of the room, but it smarted; my pride and feelings smarted more than my shoulders I admitted to myself. I must compose myself. Mother mustn't know, that was certain. She would insist on my leaving the inn, there was no other employment I could take up in this blighted area, and we must have the miniscule amount I was able to drag in each week. We would not be able to keep the house without it, or feed us all. I couldn't breathe a word of it to my siblings either, for news would travel the chain of conversation till it reached Mother. If Paulin were here still I could have talked to her. She always listened. If only she were still here, I would not have to bear the burden alone and the smarting would ease.

I stopped suddenly, the mud of the wastes sinking under my shoes, and blinked at the darkened hills leering around me. I had fancied I mourned for her these past days. I did in a way, but...this was self-pity, not mourning like for Da. The difference between the two was miles of a gap. I wasn't really mourning for

Paulin. Maybe... I had enjoyed her company more for the sake of whining about my own problems and preening my self-esteem. It might be worth considering. It might even be worth a paper[7]. I was quite thoughtful as I slogged through the mud toward home and had forgotten the smart on my shoulders. Surprisingly, one of the things that turned in my mind was the red-haired Turner Hitchley. Perhaps I should have told him about Paulin and I walking out by the south road, the night before she was found dead. She had said she saw something there earlier and wanted to see if she could spot it again when the night sun rose. We had walked far that night.

The dark was all about me. I thought for a moment there was more about, as if someone or something was on the hill above the valley which led into the path home. I paused, staring. But the black shape against the dark sky was surely just my imagination. No one ever came this direction. Dark and mud, that

---

[7] One of the main ways the fancy schools that teach teachers teach their teachers (try saying that five times fast!) is by making them write papers. At least two papers a week are due in most schools, sometimes up to five a week, and most of them are, "incorporate what is happening now in your life to tell me about such-and-such subject." Which means a student learning how to be a teacher is constantly thinking about what he can learn from his life and how it would look on paper, as he goes about his days.

characterized my life here, I thought glumly as I began to walk again, the mud pulling at my feet with each step. Except for home, of course. That was always kept bright no matter what the hour of day or even how we all felt. Mother always had a pot of cheese soup on the burner and a loaf of sweet bread for any of us who needed it, and always kept the hearth-fire burning to keep back the dark. And her heart-fires for us all too, her love never dimmed. I began to realize how different Paulin was from my courageous mother as I walked, and wondered that I had never thought of it before. Realization piled upon realization, and I understood I had never brought her home, or even mentioned her, because something in me knew Mother would see through her lovely face and honeyed words... It did seem a bit heartless to be tearing a person down after they were dead. But then it wasn't actually tearing down, it was more of comprehending who they were. Why I hadn't seen it earlier was the real mystery to me. I suppose there might be something to the theory of a pretty face clouding a man's judgment.

I was at the foot of the valley now. The two great hills rose up very high, trying to block out what tiny bits of light from the afternoon moons managed to break through the clouds. They were doing a very good job. The blackness was intensely deep through that thin valley. It had never seemed sinister to me before. But tonight it seemed to yawn like the mouth of some great monster, filled with black despair that translated itself into a black heart. I shuddered and my feet stopped moving. I stood there at the head of the valley, staring at the blackness yawning out at me, shivering a little in the still cold. I called myself all sorts of coward and fool to try and dredge up the will-power to go on. Maybe I would bypass it, and take the longer route past Master Neenbrot's farm. I turned slowly, almost as reluctant to turn my back on that yawning blackness as to go into it.

A hideous keening scream rose into the air.

No, it didn't rise.

It cut through it like a butcher knife through a flossy, slamming into me with a horror that I think quite literally made my hair stand on end; I felt my scalp prickling as the rest of me recoiled in horror. The scream was joined by a rumbling growl that shook my bones. I turned and ran, slipping and pelting back toward the main north road, the one thought in my panicking, pulsing mind to get back to town. To other people.

The scream and growl were joined by a whining howl that ran up and down the scale of my hearing and tied it all together in one horrible scream. My feet slipped and skidded through the mud as my heart shook and pounded in me. The scream followed me. No, I realized, with heart-stopping horror. It came from in front of me now. Blocking off the way to town. I spun around, my shoes sliding out from under me so I landed on my hands in the mud. I scrambled forward, getting my feet back under me with difficulty. The scream shook my insides and shrieked inside my mind.

The wailing, roaring scream shot out of the valley into my face. My legs locked in place without my telling them and I slid to a muddy stop. The darkness seemed to come at me as I stood there staring into the valley. As if it took shape from the scream and slithered toward me, shrieking out its desire to kill. My heart hammered and shook. I staggered back, aware I was gasping as I turned in a desperate circle. The scream raged all around me. I didn't think, didn't plan, I just ran. I spun and bolted for the way out of these mud flats, rushing for the road. The scream grew louder. It rose to such a pitch I could feel my eyes bulging with the pain of the noise alone. My stomach heaved and I fell to

one knee, losing my dinner and my mind reeling, everything shaking and pounding with the scream.

Something whizzed over my head. I felt the freezing air whoosh past me and back-peddled through the mud, my own scream lost in the hideous din. I could see nothing. Not even my own feet as I staggered up and threw myself at the gap between the hills again. The mud slipped and collected under my feet. It clung to me as if it was alive and holding me in place for the beast. Panic closed in as thick as the darkness. I had never had a nightmare as terrifyingly unreal as that moment, with the scream steadily debilitating me, the mud clutching at my legs, and the darkness adding its own monstrous horror. A strangled half-formed prayer jabbered from me as I rushed for the gap again.

Deeper darkness in the shape of a human rose out of the dark like a demon. I didn't even have time to scream before it was on me. The thing slammed into me, bony arms locking mine to my chest, flinging us to the mud so hard we slid yards through the thick slime. A scream ripped out of me, and I began to flail in this apparition's arms. I had to get out, I had to get out, I had to get away from the beast, from the

noise. The bony arms clutched at me, slamming me down as I jerked convulsively up. Mud gripped me, seeming to lock me in. Everything was dark shapes, stinking mud, and screaming noise that ate into my bones and mind. The thing clutching at me was yelling something as I could feel its breath. I struggled wildly, kicking and flailing. A swish of air went over us both, sharp and icy, a metal feel to it. The same sensation passed over again as I managed to jerk into a sitting position. This time it was close enough I felt it clip my hair.

"What demon are you?" I shrieked at the thing as its shoulders rammed down again, driving me back to the mud. It seemed to hold the power of air and blackness in its bony hands, whatever it was. "Jesus is stronger than the demons, Jesus is stronger than the demons," I felt myself gasping, unable to hear anything but the horrible scream that was driving me mad. I gasped it again and again into the black air as I scrabbled in the mud with this thing clutching at me. That slicing, biting blade of air cut over us again.

The scream stopped. I slammed back into the mud, my mind buzzing and my heart slamming around in my chest. My own gasps filled my hearing.

"Will you lay still now, you idiot?" Turner panted beside me. I shifted my head through the slucking mud to stare at the black figure kneeling on my chest.

"You aren't–" I started, my voice high and thin. But I broke off. My wits began to return and I would rather not admit what I had thought he was. My ears sang like all the bells of Hartsom on a holiday morn.

"They're trying to murder you!" Turner hissed at me. My ringing mind tried to catch up to the words. "It must have been something you saw on the south road, they just now figured out it was you out there with Paulin."

"South...?" I muttered feeling weak and ill. That frozen air sliced over us again, and this time I could hear the whizz of its passing. It was something thin. Something sharp. Turner hunched down over me and I heard a low exclamation come from him. "You did not really say *that*," I murmured. And then thought it was an idiotic thing to be shocked at in a moment like this. He scrambled off me. I gasped again, just lying flat in the mud, staring up at the darkness above me.

"Don't stand up. Arvi found the noisemaker and I showed him how to stop the scream, and he did. Limeny, that thing's amazing! It sticks

far down in these hills and uses the clay itself to amplify the noise – But that ain't important right now, what matters is we found it. Which means now Arvi's trying to find the thing what's slicing that blade around through the air, and it's hard without even the moons out. And these folks are experts at keeping in the shadows."

"Arvi?" I asked, struggling to my knees. I felt muzzy and muddle-headed. My stomach heaved at my actions and I doubled over, gagging out whatever was left after the last episode. I felt Turner's hand on my shoulder.

"Awful noise, ain't it?" I heard him say sympathetically, through the buzzing in my spinning mind. "Arv had us stuff cotton in our ears and I don't know when I've been so thankful for his simple sense."

"Arv?" I wheezed. Turner's arm appeared under my chin and he pointed up toward one of the hills. I followed the finger. A dark silhouette appeared on the skyline. Trim and short, a blade outstretched in their hand. It was gone again in a moment, flung down on the hill I assumed.

"Listen, Arvi can't find this guy in the dark. Well, it's taking time to find him, anyway."

"What guy?" I wheezed, my arm over my stomach. The thing, whatever it was, whizzed

over our heads again. I ducked instinctively, cold iron fear strengthening in me again. "And what is that?" I squeaked

"I ain't real sure, but I do know it's meant to cut your head off."

"What!?"

"Come on, let's see if we can help Arvi find the one what wants you dead," Turner said. He began to crawl, I could see the black lump as he moved. I slumped back in the mud with a groan and lay there, staring up at the black sky. Oh, I felt ill. And my mind buzzed like a creature with a life apart from me, spinning with too many thoughts to bring coherency. But one surfaced past the churning mass.

Someone wanted my head. Without the rest of me.

Who wanted me dead!?

Chapter 16: A Desperate Fight in the Dark or Third Encounter

Ryam sloshed back on the mud with a groan, his limbs splayed out around him. I let him lie and went to the hunting. The mud squishes under me as I run on all fours across this place, scanning everything for the guy what must be here somewhere. The leermackle's call wouldn't sound on its own.

Arvi'd found it as soon as we got close. He headed to the tallest hill, and there it was on top. A strange pillar of black metal, sitting on three thick half-moon shaped legs, with holes drilled in the pillar and wires sticking out, and an e-box on top. It's quite the impressive thing! The way the holes are placed, and with the hollowness of the thing, it's made to make lots of noise when air's blowed through it right, as it's set up to do from that e-box. But them legs! They's hollowed too and settled deep, real deep, and after a couple of kicks and a glance around at the way this place is setup I guess what they're for. These legs are made of melanchton. They's reading the earth, and sending the noise out through all three of the hills, tapping into the clay there too[8]. That was real clever of these bovys, real smart. No one's ever thought to use the metal for that. But it only took a couple glances for me to see how the box was attached, and that's how the whole thing is run.

That's when we saw Ryam running like a cornered critter. I slid down the hill to help, and left Arvi to shut the thing down by just a few instructions I hoped he heard. He had made it stop. But that pillar wouldn't have worked on its own, someone had to set it up and start it. So where was the man that was running all this?

The blade, whatever kind it was, slashed by over my head again. I ducked at the sound, my heartbeat pattering. I can't see anything in this blackness. But there has to be a way to run that blade, I realize sudden. I stop still and concentrate. For a little all I hear is the dribble of mud and Ryam's gasps and groans as he's splayed out on the mud. Then it comes again. Right over my head there's a quick swish and a rush of icy air. Then it's gone again. But it came from one side to the other side. And there ain't nobody standing right there. Even in this inky

---

[8] No, not a guess. I'm very sorry, but I have scoured the texts and find no other mention of this fascinating metal that can seemingly "read the earth" and communicate with like things. I do wish we could find a more reliable way to speak to those on Planistah, and ask them questions. Boxes that hop randomly through time are only so much good.

blackness I can tell that much. Which means this person has to be on one of the hills rising beside me, in order to make his blade run the length it is.

I turn and start to shimmy toward the hill on my right. The mud slips and oozes as I set a foot on it and a grunt comes from me as I slide right back down. That swish comes again. From right over me, so close the air of it shifts my hair around on my head. I slide down farther on the mud, feeling shaky sudden and my stomach a little sick. Truth, looks like I wouldn't be clambering up anything. I slump with my head on my knees and consider. I can't go up the hill. I can't go under it. A clap of thunder goes over us, rumbling, and lightning follows right on its heels. Ryam jerks up like someone set off a spring behind him and sits there with mud dripping from him in the bright white light. It dies and the darkness and quiet seem even deeper. Then another slap of thunder and flash of lightning come. This time I see Arv. He's on the hill right across from me, crouched down with his black hood over his head, searching through the scene for this guy. Sudden I realize with the thunder and lightning following so close, it means the lightning's ready to strike. Somewhere right near us. Arvi's got his

klackmen out up there on top one of the highest hills.

"Blank!" I muttered, and winced at it. Every time I think I've got that habit licked...

"What is it?" Ryam squeaks at me.

"We have to find this guy, and get Arvi off that hill! Ryam, listen, this blade is coming slantwise, always over our heads from north to south—"

"A line running from the tops of the hills," Ryam buts in. He's a smart one, even if he does get a little squeaky under pressure. "We can't go up the hill without getting our heads chopped off, and it isn't possible to go under them. You go out toward the south road, I'll go through the valley, and we will see if we can circle around and spot this murderer."

"Right," I say, a little surprised that he's snapped into his senses so fast. "Don't stand up!"

"I am not that much of an idiot," he mutters. I see his black shape go shuffling toward the left as he scuttles on all fours toward the real dense black of the valley. I shift, mud oozing under me with every move, and start to scuttle along the opposite way. I hear the swish coming again. But this time it's at my ear. I fling myself to the mud, face-slamming it, and the splash of the muck sailing up nearly drowns out the sound of the swish. Near, but not quite. It goes over once, then almost immediately swishes back again, along the same line but the opposite direction. Mud slucks as I lift my head up, gasping out thanks to the Maker. That were close. Too close, way too close. I barely heard it before it was there, and if I hadn't have heard it...well, I'd be about a half foot shorter now. This guy whoever he is, has figured out how to make his line go just a few inches lower. A few inches is enough.

I shift my elbows forward in the mud, flex my knees, and start to sort of swim through the mud. The land is tilting up. That's what it is, not that the guy could make his line lower, but that the land is going up. I feel myself shaking as I keep shuffling forward. I swallow hard and stay down as I crawl, everything focused on my hearing, listening for that deadly swish with all I's got in me.

Thunder claps and I jump so hard I face-slam again with the rebound. I come up gasping and spitting out the mud. Lightning strikes on a hill in front of me. I see it come down and the sizzle as it hits the wet mud, about two blocks from us. I start shuffling faster. Arvi's gotta get down from there. But he won't until we find this person what's got Ryam and me pinned. I slide forward fast, slithering through the mud and for once glad it's so slippery. I wasn't sure what I could do, and I was wracking my brains as I slithered forward. But mostly I was listening, with my heart pounding away, for that swishing sound. This place was going uphill still. Which meant that line could reach down farther. It came again, that swish, right over my head. It was sure following me. And awful close. It were definitely following me.

I lay still again and thought. If I could figure out how it worked, maybe I could figure a way around it. Thunder cracked again. Lightning followed right after, sizzling on a hill somewhere to our left. I could hear the snap and sizzle going with the light even from where I lay. That was getting closer too. My mind whirled, ignoring my headache and the muck and cold. It had to be a blade running on some sort of wire system. One man operated it, which told me it was a slick setup, where they's had to know where their victim would walk, and set it up beforehand, because the sides would have to be on opposite hills. All right, now when a wire system ran and something ran along it, the shortest part of the curve was...where it started to turn. I was in the middle now, the lowest point. I shoved my elbow hard into the mud and started to roll left, near frantically. That shing came again. But this time it was a little less, like it were just a bit higher than it had been the last time. Wet mud sloshed against my side as I banged up against the hillside. So far I's doing fine. I flipped on my back and waited.

That swish came again, right above me. I waited still. I heard the sound of it coming, then it whizzed on past me with the backstroke. My hand shot up, waving in the air, frantically looking for it. Cold metal fibers brushed against my fingers. I'd found the wire. The whine came again and I jerked my hand down, throat closing in terror. Something ice cold, thin as a wafer, and sickening sharp, ran along the tops of my curled fingers. I hissed and pulled them closer, feeling warm blood on my frozen hand. Thunder clapped again.

"Arv, aytem!" I screamed up at the night, holding my breath. Lightning flashed just above us. My hand shot up and pointed where I knew the wire hung down. "Here!"

The light died. I heard air whistling. One was the swish, that deadly horror headed back with the backstroke. The other was a humming whine what I'd heard ever since I met my pal. I jerked onto my side, flinging myself in a roll, trying desperate to get out of the way. A metallic

crack, like a metal whip, rang in the air, then a whirring swish, and something thin-sounding went "zing" and "splat."

Thunder rolled again and I jerk up scrabbling to get my feet under me as the mud slips and that warm keeps rolling from my hand. I set my boot on the hill, the mud caves, and I tumble down with a little cry, landing smack on my hurt fingers. Things go dizzy again for a second. White light cuts through the black night as I hear another burst of lightning sizzle and pop and my hair dances on my scalp. I jerk up again and scramble for the hill. I got to find this bovy what's trying to murder us all, or Arvi's like to be toasted.

Chapter 17: Strange Danger or The Adversary Met

Thunder clapped again, rolling through the hill lands as a bansin drum roll. I dropped to my belly to offer as much resistance as possible to the sliding mud, and to be certain I was not the highest point upon this lump of clay. Yet Peace wouldst be like to draw the bolt. If he did not, the black tower of wires and metal beside me wouldst. I had found the leermackle's scream. It rested upon this hilltop, jammed into the mud with its three half-moon, thick black legs. With it I found the answer to the riddle of the holes in the hill. But I had stood staring at the thing, unable to guess what to do next. It was Turner who had run his clever hands over the strange pillar and nigh immediately pointed out the box upon the top and a single wire out of the eight running from the thing. He had disappeared thereafter, rushing headlong back the way we came to aid his new-found friend, unable to hear my yells to stop and wait. Now the beast was silent. But our forces were split, and danger couldst strike at two places instead of one.

A bolt of lightning shot from the sky, dazzling my eyes. Speaking of danger striking...

It was very close. Yet I couldst not leave the hilltop, for from here I had a vantage point to see all the area. I must find this villain striving to take the lads' lives, before he managed to arrange another of his infernal wires. I had seen it. For an instant, when Turner shouted but a moment hence and the lightning lit the scene. A slim, dark line running from hill to hill, while a disc-like metal blade shone rushing back at my young friend as he lay upon the mud and pointed to the line.

Lightning pierced through the blackness as a bolt struck the hill just beyond mine. My skin prickled and hair danced, but I heeded it not. I was desperately seeking to see two things; a live Turner and an enemy. Turner I spotted immediately, he was sliding back down from an attempted rush at the hill. My peripheral vision seemed to catch something black upon the top of Turner's mud hill. But the light died, and it was come and gone so quickly I couldst not be sure. Lying here was doing little good. And it would summon the lightning till I was but a charred body lying upon this hilltop. I must do something before the next bolt sailed from the sky. I gained my feet and ran across the hilltop, keeping low.

The unmistakable whine of an arrow shaft

shot past my arm. I flung myself forward, aiming for the edge of the hill. If this villain couldst aim that close even after I hadst left my earlier position, he had the capability of seeing through the darkness. These people had created very odd objects. I well believed some new infernal design lay in his hands; and it could prove deadly to us. A way to see through the darkness! This changed the battle. Now that we had destroyed his ability to slice off a man's head he was diverging into more well-known techniques. But an arrow had more range than their Leermackle wire. The battle had shifted, indeed.

The world was black, with a mass of deeper black seeming to reach out for me from the mud of the hill. My left shoulder rammed into the mud, spurting it up in a fountain that covered me. I began to slide, slipping off the side of the hill, gathering momentum as I went. Mud filled my world. It caught at my legs and held them fast as in a weight. My ears, throat, nose, all of it was filled with the oozing stench-filled mud as I slid, faster and harder. The weight of the mud built. It was engulfing me. A sudden horror overcame me, like unto that which used to come on me in the presence of water (and still does on occasion, though since the boat upon the Muers river, in recovery with Turner and Aston, its horror had faded). My arms flailed, breaking through the clay, as I struggled to cast off the weight. I couldst feel my lungs beginning to ache and strive for breath within me, and it brought the panic to new heights. With a furiously beating heart and a burst of mighty energy, I jerked upright, staggering to my feet. A roar burst from me and I felt my klemnins leap into my hands. A sharp exclamation, nigh a squeak, sounded in front of me, almost beneath my feet. I staggered backward, blowing hard and attempting to shake the clay from my face.

"Great cheese cakes, I thought you were a mud demon set on dragging me to the lake!" a young voice gasped, my own panic echoing in his voice. I shook myself, like unto Mel when he comes from a bath, and was able to see again. Black shapes were the extent of my vision. Yet there was a darker shape near under my feet that I thought me was in the form of a young man. "Don't go leaping out on a person like that, unless you want a scholar's heart-attack on your hands!" Ah, Master Ryam, Turner's new acquaintance.

"My pardon," I gasped, wishing for one little corner of clean clothing with which to clear my

face. "Do not go into the open. Our enemy has a way of seeing through the darkness."

"We cannot stay on the hill or we will be struck by lightning," the boy mused, "and we cannot rush at him without his seeing and shooting us. How are we to catch the man?" I did not answer, for I was still shaking off mud and striving to calm the panic. A hand reached from the darkness and clamped upon my arm. I resisted the urge to let the panic return and chop through the wrist with a klemnin. Though it took an effort and a deal of mental discipline to convince myself it was this Ryam and no villain reaching to pull me back into the mud.

"Mud! Lovely, perfect mud!" the lad exclaimed in excitement.

"There is enough about for thee," I stated, a bit cautiously. Had he taken a knock to the head this evening?

"No, listen, if we roll ourselves in mud, as you have already done, and stay very close to the hills, we will be nearly invisible to any watcher!"

"Oh." That seemed a sound idea. As sound as any I couldst contrive in any case. "Do you avail yourself of the method, then make thy way toward Turner. Thou must inform him of the murderer's ability to see through the dark for he is in grave danger. An enemy's skill is especially dangerous when it is unknown."

I turned without more words and began to make my way swiftly around the hill, feeling my way with a hand upon the mud of this hillside. My boots slipped and slid, striving to throw me down with each step, as I staggered around the hill. It was difficult to rush under such circumstances. But Turner was out within sight of this villain. I found my heart fighting within me as images flashed across my soul; this past year of solitary journeys, Turner's impish smile, and the solitude staying forever. It had not crossed my consciousness that I was lonely. Yet in that moment of creeping in the dark, mud sliding everywhere and thunder rolling, I knew I had missed my little friend as surely as this mud smelled foul.

A man tends to recognize how much he values a thing when he is in danger of losing it.

Turner knew not of this inhuman ability to see through the blackness and wouldst not guard against it. Any moment might be his last. I reached the end of my hill, where it diverged into sight of where this monstrous murderer hunted, and pressed myself against the hillside, striving to keep my boots under me.

Another lightning bolt lit the scene. This

came as a set of three separate flashes following upon each other's heels. The thunder rolled around me, echoing in and out of the hills till it seemed to be a constant assault. In the first flash I spied Turner, beginning to make his way up the hillside toward where this murderer stood, and the lumpish form in the mud that I knew must be Master Ryam, sneaking his way closer to my friend. The second flash showed an infinitesimally slim rod stretched between that hill and mine, wherein I guessed the deadly bladed wire attached. Then came the third flash, the thunder rolling behind it. My eyes were riveted upon the opposite hill, as I willed them not to shrink back from the sudden furious light.

A black form stood silhouetted against the dark sky. I couldst see little of the man, except to note his cloak billowed and a bow was pointed down, toward where Turner scrambled up the hill. My hand shot up with an aytem. No thought went into that shot. It was all a swift instinct, a shot hurled with a heart that hammered in fear and dread of losing Turner Hitchley, and furious anger at this monster who wouldst slay a boy. I couldst not let that happen. My silver star was off before the flash of light died away.

The heavens opened and rain began to pour.

It was a dark, frozen, heavy rain. My mouth pressed together and I pushed off my hill, dropping to the ground and proceeding in a swimming slither through the thickening downpour as it churned the mud under me. God help us, my shot wouldst have been diverted. The rain was heavy enough, and sudden enough, to interfere with its impetus and its aim! If the arrow from that bow loosed... Surprise and secrecy be hanged. I yelled for Turner, shouting for him to gain cover and leave off his mad charge. But I couldst barely hear my own voice. The rain muffled everything and the mud bubbled and churned under the waters. I could not see him to drag him off, could not be heard to warn him. There was no time left to reach Turner. In but a moment he would be dead if I did not intervene. I deserted stealth. The rain washed away my muddy disguise in any case. My feet slammed into the mud and I ran. Body low, feet pounding, everything concentrated on gaining that hill and wresting the weapons from my foe, this inhuman beast, threatening to slay a boy for naught but personal gain.

I must change that bow's aim!

I slammed into the hill, eyes closed against

the downpour. My hands bit into the mud as the toes of my boots jammed through the muck, and I clawed my way up. Rivers of mud ran beside me, under me, and even over me as I scrambled and fought my way upward. It was a suicidal maneuver and I knew it. This man had every advantage, and I couldst not even see him unless I reached a certain point. But if I did not draw his aim, Turner would die. The rain pounded into me, swallowing all other sounds in its roar, and freezing me with its fury. On I scrambled, scaling that hill with a burning anger driving me on. I had no cover, and used no stealth. But it would distract from Turner, and if I couldst be the saving of him it was enough.

Searing pain slammed through my left side. It drove me backward with the force. My wits froze with the shock, but only for an instant. I was but yards the top when I felt the red-hot pain of the arrow embedding itself deep in me through the top of my shoulder. But it was the murderer's undoing. Instantly I analyzed the angle, as I jerked my hand up with an aytem cupped in my palm. My weapon loosed. I couldst hear it slashing through the rain as it spun on its way, sending spray hither and yon.

A death cry rang through the night. A

human's hideous howl of pain and hopeless terror, as they knew their last moments had come. It faded, lost in the midst of the drowning rain and churning mud. Thunder roared and echoed around us. A lightning bolt landed some half mile from us, as the storm rolled to the east. A black form, arching backward and crumpling toward the muddied ground, was silhouetted in the white light of the flash. A groaning sigh slid from me as the mud took over. My boots slipped out from under me and I slammed into the mud river. The impact broke the arrow shaft. I heard a roar emerge from me as a blackness from within overtook the blackness of the night.

Chapter 18: Another Corpse or Morning

I saw Arvi fall. In the flash of that lightning bolt all I saw was an arrow sticking out of Arvi and him falling face first in the mud of the hill. The flash died and the death scream came. I heard myself gasping out nonsense as I jerked forward, feeling my way to where I knew the mud would carry him down. I didn't think about the murdering bovy up there, or about nothing, just praying desperate, babbling nonsense. For Arvi to be all right, for that arrow not to have killed him off. Why had he run headfirst into it? Arvi was smarter than that, why hadn't he watched himself! My foot rammed into something and I went head first over it into the mud. But it was a soft something. I jerked up again and reached back. A slimed, muddied tunic met my hand. I gripped it and pulled. A slucking sound, loud enough to be heard over the pounding rain, rewarded my efforts. I heard a sharp, deep inhalation and knew Arvi was breathing again after that mud slide. I reached blind for his shoulder. And the cold weren't just outside me from the rain no more. That arrow had to have come at near point blank range, with that guy

on the hill top. With force like that...

The top of it was broken off. I could feel where the shaft went in, right next to his neck, and even the barest tip, but the feathers and all were long gone. I ran a hand down his slimed tunic, where I knew the arrow had to have traveled from the angle of it still sticking out the top, wondering desperate how far in it went. My hand stopped at his side, about four inches from his arm socket. An arrow head stuck out here. I didn't think about it. I didn't even think if it were best to do it there or wait till we got him back to town. I just grabbed that thing and pulled.

Arvi jerked up with a roar, swiping at my head with one of his gollywompers. I caught his wrist and shot an arm around his shoulders as he started to slump back toward the ground again.

"It's me, Arv," I yelled over the rain. "It's me, it's all right." But I weren't sure it was. The mud around the two of us was warm and thick as it swirled, and I knew Arvi was losing more blood than he could handle. I jerked my tunic off and held it into the rain pour, willing it to wash some of the stinking mud off. I only did that for a few seconds though, afore I was shoving it in Arvi's side, trying to stop the bleeding. It was

soaking fast. Too fast. I needed something bigger, something I could tie around it. I heard someone stagger up and glanced over to see Ryam's thin form beside me. "Your cloak!" I yelled over the rain. "Let me use your cloak, Arvi's losing too much blood, we gotta' staunch its flow!" He gasps out something in answer, but I don't hear it over the rain. A sopping cloak comes flapping out of the dark and slaps me in the face. I grabbed it, rolled it into a log, and started in, shoving part of it in Arv's wound and tying the rest around so's it covered both points where the arrow stuck out. The mud slucked again as I shoved myself on Arvi's side, pushing him over so's his wound was up and I had the leverage to put some decent pressure on it. I stayed like that, breathing hard, feeling the cloak warming and smelling that sick, sweet iron even through the downpour.

I leaned there, shivering in the roaring rain, and praying silent.

Things were going gray instead of black, I noticed sudden. The sun was thinking about coming up. After a few minutes the rain started to ease up. It got slower and lighter, and as it did the place got lighter and lighter. I could see Ryam, huddled against the hill, hugging his knees and looking like he might forfeit as he stared at Arv and me. I could see the thin pole sticking across the two hills, and even the wire hanging off of it, though the ends were lost in the mud somewhere. And I could see Arvi. He was desperate pale, and out proper, his face all splattered with mud, as he lay there under my hands. All sudden it was like I was on board that ship of Black's again. With Arvi crazed and near dead, and me terrified and hurtin' and more lonely than I's ever been. I shuddered in the cold, closed my eyes to the scene, and let all of that pour out in a prayer. The simple type, because when yourn really upset, that's what comes out of you. The fancy prayers, with all the high theology and long-winded prose, those are fine, real fine. But they aren't what you pray when your best pal is bleeding to death in a mud waste and all you can do is watch. Those kinds of prayers are simple, repeat a lot, and you remember how God spoke through *them* long after the fancy ones are dead and forgotten. Sometimes I wondered if that's why God lets us have times that wrench our souls. We remember those prayers. The rain left and the sky turned from black, to gray, to gold, to blue.

"Is he dead?" Ryam muttered, his voice hoarse. It was the first time we'd spoke in near an hour.

"He's breathing," I murmured back. "I think... I think the blood's stopped coming for good now." It had stopped, then started, then stopped again during that hour. Now I sat back on my heels, letting my breath blow out.

"What do we do now?" Ryam asked.

"You go on home, or to town, whichever is closer. Get help. We need a cart to get Arvi to the doctor." Fool, why hadn't I sent him off for that before?

"What about that one?" Ryam asked, and pointed. I followed his finger and saw the back of a cart sticking out from the hill. Maybe that was... I glanced at Arvi again, but he were out solid, the bleeding had stopped, and he seemed to be breathing all right. I hopped up and trotted toward the cart. If it could be called that.

The upper half was a normal cart, a simple seat at the front of a wooden rectangle, with plank sides what rose up about four feet to keep things from falling out as it rolled. But the rest of it weren't normal. Two big old wooden cylinders were stuck on the bottom of the thing. They were massive, probably whole tree trunks, real carefully made into what we saw here. A square of metal rods ran around the bottom of the cart, with more metal rods running through the center of the cylinders and back up the cart, connecting it all, and allowing the two huge logs to roll when this thing was pulled. A lean, sad looking merthyl turned its head to look at me, where it was harnessed to the front of this thing. I stuck a hand on the back of the cart and pushed. It shifted easily, rising a foot before rolling back to settle again. It was well-fashioned and a real nice piece of workmanship. But I was inclined to hate the thing. It was obvious this was how they made their leermackle tracks and it had been used by awful folks, to murder and lie to a whole town. But I didn't shade myself, the real reason I hated it was because I knew I had been in a trip in it before, and it hadn't been a nice one.

"I ain't sure about taking Arvi in this, wounded like he is," I said, remembering how sick it made me to go up and down, and that with just a headache. It would be worse wounded like he was. Instead I shoved a finger in my mouth and whistled for Kleof, where we left him a hill or two over. "You take Arvi's merthyl and ride into town, get the doctor and whoever he needs to come on out with his cart."

"How will I get them to come?" Ryam asked, a little panic in his voice as he stared at Kleof trotting up. He had to stretch his neck to see the war merthyl's head when Kleof was next to him.

"Just tell 'em Arvi's name and offer them a purse for their trouble. That should get as many volunteers as we need," I grunted as I helped Ryam scramble onto Kleof's back.

"What is his name?" Ryam gasped as he grabbed a handful of neck feathers to keep himself up.

"Arvimeer Aytenmar, Chief Courtier and Protector of the King. Town, Kleof, back to the inn!"

Ryam's mouth hung open as Kleof took off, pounding over the wet mud toward town. But I didn't stand there staring after them. I ran back to Arvi. He was still just lying there, all pale and still. But he was breathing steady and not too strained. His wounds seem to have clotted for sure, no more fresh blood stained anything. I sat back on my heels. The waiting closed in again. I could hear the mud sliding and settlings. After a few minutes, my eyes drifted back to the parked cart. It was a fascinating bit of workmanship. And that leermackle call was even more impressive. I had never seen anything like these. I wanted to get a closer look at what else these people might have. A glance at Arv showed it wouldn't make no difference to him if I stayed beside him just now.

I set a boot on the hill, then another. I slid,

but not as much as last night, when I was trying to go up the steepest side, in the dark, in a rush. I could climb it now. Arvi had managed it last night. Why had he done that? Even in the pitch dark a guy could see someone running at him when he was two yards away! He must have known it would like to kill him. He would have known. He did know! I was frowning hard as I scrambled up that hill, ruminating on that stupid move of Arv's, when he really weren't one to make stupid moves, ever. Sure he might not be the first one to come up with a brilliant scheme, but he was smart. Not just stuffed with knowledge, I mean real smarts that could think on their own. Especially when it came to battle knowledge, he never slipped up there.

Until now. Why had he rushed the hill like that?

Sunlight slanted into my face and I jerked back, my heart pounding in me. I had gotten to the crest without realizing it, and just stuck my head up there for anybody to wallop off or send an arrow through. Now that, that was a stupid move. That's what comes of fretting over things I couldn't understand. I crouched on the hill side for thirty full seconds, feeling my heart beating hard in me, listening. There wasn't a sound. I slowly stuck my head up again. There

was somebody there all right. Or maybe the remains of what used to be somebody would be a better way to put it. What was left of him didn't have the thing we call life, that makes you call it a someone. Anyway, he were sure dead. I scrambled up the rest of the way and took a look around in the sunlight.

I could see the black pillar on the hill opposite. It shone a little in the sun, the wires waving in the gentle breeze. Real innocent looking. It was hard to believe it could be deadly, just by the sound it made. But right in front of me was a black pole, and that interested me more. It were attached to another pole, real thin, what stretched across to the opposite hill, where still another pole stood. I could see the ends of the black wire hanging off each corner of this thing. I reached out my hand, the caked blood cracking on my knuckles and sending a little line of fire through my arm. It was cold metal, and it didn't move when I pushed it. I took a closer look. Up at the corner, where the thin pole joined with the one connected to my hill, there was a slim handle. I reached up for it and found it had a trigger just inside. It was smooth and awful cold when I wrapped my fingers round it, but I didn't mind, and just tightened my hold. It didn't want to move. I reached up my other hand and squeezed with both. The trigger went down with a snap, and sudden the pole under my hands would move where I shoved it. And when I shoved it, the one on the opposite hill moved too. It were pretty heavy, but if I wanted I could have run it the whole length of this hill. Another trigger was under the first one I used, but that didn't take any figuring. It was attached to the ruined wire and was how the guy released the blade when it weren't broke. Well this one was simple enough. Not much like the clever noisemaker back on the other hill. It had a short command of the area too, as soon as your target moved out of the valley, they were out of your reach.

As I played with the poles, my boot rammed into something. I looked down and gagged. I was nearly on top what was left of this guy. But I mastered myself fast, and looked back at what I had kicked. It was lying next to his hand, and at first glance it looked like two spy-glasses wired together. I picked it up and turned it over in my hands. The front of them weren't ordinary shaped glass. It looked like the sightless stares of the dead squackers what Quinty came bringing up to the house so proudly some days. It looked just like those. I turned it around and put it to my eyes. I could

see through them, where the mud hadn't splattered. Not any better than usual. But a squacker could see about the same as us. 'Cept it could– I stopped short, my mind seeming to freeze in me. I grabbed this guy's cloak, ignoring the patches of sticky red wet, and tossed it over my head. I snapped the glasses up and stared through them.

The world came to me in a yellow glow. I could see my feet, even make out the different patterns in the mud. I could see every hair on my hand when I held it out, and the lines in the caked blood where it had cracked. These didn't just look like a squacker, they looked like a squacker! I mean, someone had taken a squacker's eyes, and made these glasses out of it. These were preserved squackers eyes as lenses, and with it I could see in the dark! And I could see why Arvi had made that desperate run. He had known about this. He had known I didn't know, and that I was about to get shot down by a bovy what could see in the dark as good as any monster.

Arvi had made that run to draw the fire from me.

Chapter 19: The Way Home or Conclusion

Strangers gripped my shoulders. Images of the Cranson bandits and their dealings with their enemies filled my mind, and panic seized me. I jerked, striving to release myself from their unknown grasp. Deep, deep pain pierced me. I slumped back, my reeling mind dimming as my strength proved unequal to the task of moving. Yet the panic grew as I was lifted higher.

Another pair of hands slid in with my captors, supporting my lolling head. Turner. I knew those thin, calloused hands. The panic rolled off. My breathing steadied. I let the blackness close in again.

Vague images of a sling between two pack merthyls invaded my consciousness. But the pain thundered and brought a blackness which constantly took over. Voices came and went. Most were a dull background roar that I could not understand, an accompaniment to the roar of the black pain. Sometimes I heard discussions of monies, with Turner ever being the haggler. Once I heard the innkeeper shout in anger at my friend. Instinct drove me to propel myself upright, to protect him. Again

came that hot, debilitating pain and weakness. It eclipsed all else.

The night-terrors returned. The curse of the Aytenmars, ever nightmares had plagued me, but with a severe wounding the residual effects of the ockthain came upon me; it bid the dreams escalate to something beyond mere nightmares. All I knew was blackness, terror, and pain. Drowning, all I loved slain, the villains and monsters with leave to slay me slowly, and slay me yet again. Screams filled all my hearing and seemed all I knew. Nay, but sometimes during this season I also knew Turner. A vaguely understood, certain source of safety. Even a comfort of sorts. But though he lessened the intensity he could not dispel the monsters that ripped, the deaths that I watched and felt, again and yet again. It might have been a day I spent thus, it might have been ten days. But I think me, by God's good grace, it was but a short time. The dreams began to fade to a state of semi-conscious drowsy contentment. I understood very little of what was around me. But I was pleased by all the world.

I did not wake in truth for what must have been some time. It was the sun shining in my eyes which brought me to that wakefulness. It took a moment to force my eyes open. When I did, I saw my room in the inn. Bright sunlight spilled through the single window, forcing its way around an impossibly wide fellow, with his back turned to me.

"Servant Meagan?" I murmured, striving to decipher if I was indeed awake or still in some state of dreams. The chief knight turned from where he had been looking out the window, and looked upon me.

"You are finally awake. Good. You did a great deal here," he rumbled. Shouldst I apologize for the work load laid upon him? I couldst hear his heavy steps against the flooring as he crossed to drop into a chair beside my bed. His elbows rested upon his knees and he regarded me with his wise, steady gaze. "Why did you run head on at him?"

"The enemy couldst see in the dark and Turner knew it not. I had to draw his aim or Turner wouldst have been another victim of the ersatz leermackle," I murmured. My throat felt gritty and thick.

"Turner said as much," Meagan nodded. "As he waved some sort of dual glasses in my face and spouted on about squackers."

"Where...?" I murmured, finding it difficult to speak. His great hand slid under me, propping me upon two pillows, and I found a

clay mug pressed to my lips. Hot peppermint tea, infused with healing herbs, slid into me. It eased my throat at once and gave my mind a semblance of vigor again.

"Sleeping." Meagan's large hand waved toward the other bed and I saw a familiar red tousled head poking out the top of the covers. "He hadn't at all since you tried to kill yourself. When I got here this morning I found him bloodshot and nearly in tears, thinking he had killed you by coming. Be better after some sleep. Counterfeiters?"

"Yes," I murmured, and tried to sit up. That proved merely I was unfit for it. I slumped back with a groan, my eyes sparking at the pain. It seemed I wouldst not be leading the way to the men we had left bound in the mud wastes. "A cave, off the south road," I muttered, and gave the chief knight the best method of finding the place once more. He nodded, patted my shoulder, and left. I heard the key turn in the lock, let my head droop farther into the pillows, and allowed myself a groan. It was a great annoyance to be wounded. Sleep came again and I let it.

The next two weeks were spent in much the same way, save the times I awoke lengthened as the days came and my body healed itself. There was a healer in town, but he was hardly adequate. Turner and I both sent him packing for his ill crafted wares and ignorant practices. Servant Meagan stayed the whole of those weeks, delving deeper into this matter of murders and counterfeiters and an entire town complicit with it. Nay, not the whole town. Only most of the merchants and business owners, out to make a profit they had not earned, and willing to take a large amount of counterfeit money in place of a smaller amount of real gold. Foolish man, thy heart loves gain so much, thou lose what thou hast in hopes of acquiring more! There is little else that canst be said of such fools. At the end of the fortnight, the three of us quit the town of Peyson, with over a score of people incarcerated and at least four already tried for murder and sentenced to hang.

Servant Meagan relished the work. Many in Peyson thought him a cold-hearted judge salivating to see justice wreaked upon men. I knew it to be the simple joy of a servant let loose from paperwork long enough to be back in the field for a brief time.

I remember little of the trip back. I was either sleeping or raving. I recall little of my ravings either, save that later Turner told me I reverted again into the "peaceful green" as he

terms my recurring mind-illness (recurring only with heavy sickness or a dire wound, I am blessed to say). When I truly came to myself, I was lying upon a small day bed in a brightly lit rounded room, and something was creating a dull ache in my stomach area. Slapping on it. My mind became a trifle clearer, the buzzing in my ears receded, and I was able to hear the sound accompanying the slapping. Aston was singing.

"My dog eats his swad[9] and sleeps and sleeps." He repeated it in his droning, tuneless manner, the same words over and over. I blinked hard and focused with an effort. The boy stood beside me as I lay on a cot, a cooking spoon in his hand which he slapped into my stomach, apparently to keep the rhythm for his song.

"Aston, no!" Corinth's voice interrupted him, and her arms loomed into view, scooping up the high prince and chiding him in a quiet tone. I felt myself chuckling, and though it burned my wound, it was worth the effort.

"I mind not the little one's play," I croaked.

---

[9] I have tried to translate this word, I tried very hard. But after careful work and continuous study, I have come to believe it is, in fact, babbling from a three-year-old. Perhaps his own form of "salad," as that is what he was interested in the last time we met the young fellow.

"He has an innate rhythm, he shall be a worthy musician one day." Corinth plopped the child upon the ground again and was on her knees beside me in a moment, studying my features and offering me water and broths. I slept soon after that. When I woke the shadows were deep, and Turner sat beside my cot, his mathematics book upon his knees. He smiled up at me when he heard me stirring.

"I was beginning to think you'd sleep till the next moons at least," he commented.

"How long since we returned to Hartsom?" I yawned.

"Three days. Mrs. Hartsom wouldn't let you come home with just me, so yourn been in Aston's room, where she can help look after you."

"Did Astor Meagan finish the business of the cave and the villains therein?"

"Truth yes. Fact I just got a letter from Ryam this morning and the whole region's turning out to see that cave his da dug out. It's turning out to be a real big thing. His da is getting lots of praise for it and it sounds like that's making Ryam and his family happy."

"Good," I said. There didn't seem to be anything else to add. Turner smiled at me again and went back to his math. We stayed thus, he

studying and I idly watching the shadows change. Nigh an hour after I drifted peacefully back to sleep.

I woke often after that, and was well enough to rise alone after three more days had passed. Though Corinth would not let me often. It would have been a wearisome time indeed, except Aston and his little siblings were about. It was certainly not dull. No home with young children can be dull. Sometimes it is hectic, sometimes worrisome, sometimes even angering. But it is most oft merry, and always blessed.

A week after I found myself in Aston's rooms, I was ready to retire to my own quarters. But I somewhat dreaded broaching the subject with Corinth. She is a nurse with very adamant ideas. That day I sat upon their rooftop, for the stable roof is flat, with a rail running around the top. The Hartsoms had made it into their personal porch, and an enclosed play area for the children upon fair days. It was a fair day today, for the sun shone brightly in a blue sky, and only a few clouds obscured the daylight (a rare thing in Hartsom, where a sky entirely obscured by clouds was the normality). Charlie lounged next to me, dandling his son on his knee in an infrequent moment of peace. Mel snored happily upon the king's feet. The dog had grown portly these last years, and resembled nothing so much as a fuzzy sausage link, rather ill stuffed. Corinth sat near my chair, dividing toys into their proper baskets as Aston gleefully snatched the items up again. Maysee managed to roll and overturn a full basket.

"Did you ever find out what Turner had done with the guardsmen?" Corinth asked, as she gathered up toys again.

"He had created what he terms 'a band,' to rescue those who were in need from the dark ways' nooners," I answered. Another basket overturned with a clatter of rattles and squeaks; but this time it was Corinth's own hand, she started so.

"He was what?" she nearly yelled.

"Fear not, he has promised me to disband the gang and not to go about it again," I told her easily. She stared at me, as if waiting.

"And?" the queen prodded after a moment.

"There is nothing else to add," I said, a bit hesitantly.

"Didn't you at least tell him not to go back into the dark ways? It is too dangerous!" she said, still staring upon me.

"Oh, I shouldst not fret over such a matter,"

I said, leaning back again and glad I could ease her mind. "He is a resourceful lad, whom I trust to keep his wits and come safe away from most any situation."

"And that was the end of the matter?" Corinth asked, seeming almost astonished.

"Of course," I said, wondering why she asked it.

"You aren't, I suppose, going to monitor his movements particularly?" she asked, and I almost thought there was a wistful note to it.

"We have an unspoken agreement; I do not often inquire into his doings, and he keeps up with his schooling and himself out of serious harm," I answered. "It suits us well, for we both have independence and trust."

A slow, merry chuckle came from Charlie.

"I think, Coorinth, tha Lord knew what He was doing when He gave Turner into Arvi's care and not ours. Coome now, Arvi, tell me about this leermackle business. I 'ave been too busy to gathah tha details," he requested, lounging back in the sunshine with his son blissfully asleep on his father's chest. I did so, and ended it with a simple statement that I was now well. Corinth snorted, but Charlie grinned lazily at her.

"I am well enough to return home," I added, almost plaintively. It was a merry thing to spend time with the young princes and princess, and my cousins. But there comes a time when one longs for one's own bed and the joy of gathering things from thine own larder. Corinth merely snorted again. But Charlie took up for me, in his gentle, peace-making manner, and it is rare he does not get his way when he chooses to speak his mind. I was allowed to descend and walk home that evening, with Charlie beside me to see I arrived safe and well. My cousin stayed for nigh an hour, until Turner returned from his afternoon at the Trosks. We spoke of many things, and of nothing at all. It was a rare time for both of us, to have an hour of peace to ourselves, and very welcome.

But when Turner returned I was quite weary, and slept near twenty hours. The next day I was more whole than I had yet been, and able to take up my morning exercises. A week after that I reported to Servant Meagan to inform him I was available for use again. He was right glad to hear it.

As I strode into our glen, Turner looked up from where he was attempting to wrest his grammar book from Quinty's wide jaws (he must have spilt creamed fruit upon the book again). His eyes locked on the sheaf of papers in my hand and his face fell. He looked back at his

dragon almost immediately and the disappointment was absent as I stepped up beside him.

"So, looks like Meagan had a lot stacked up for you to do. Where yourn off to first?"

"'You are,' Turner. Though in this instance even that is not quite the correct grammar to encompass the situation. Gather thy books and see if Layah can feed thy naughty dragon for thee, we leave in but an hour." His freckled face lit as with a sun brightening within. He shot into a cartwheel as I stepped inside to begin to gather traveling gear.

"I don't guess you'd tell me why I'm coming, would you?" Turner asked brightly, sticking his head in the kitchen window. I paused in my gathering stores, for just an instant. Shouldst I tell him the full truth? I wouldst not have him endangered and alone, and I wouldst rather not have myself alone either. It was better to be endangered together, where one might rescue the other. That is the way of brothers.

"You were of *some* use in Jaspur. It might be I shall need an errand runner."

"For you? Not likely," Turner grinned. I made no answer, but only turned with a smile to continue gathering stores. We would see little enough sources to purchase items in the wild

lands where we traveled this day. Yet the lonely places wouldst not be lonely. For either of us. We would bear each other's foul moods and jests, and ever watch the other's back. For that too is the way of brothers. We would have need to guard one another before this task was done. Yes. It would be well to have Turner along.

"Layah ain't around, and Tilmey can't keep a dragon where he's living now," Turner called in through the window again. "We's gonna have to take Quinty with us." My smile froze. I looked down at the Vector stink dragon. She looked back at me. A toothy smile spread over her face, and I swear she was taking joy in my discomfiture. Hm. There would be much to bear from each other's company. Never mind the brigands we went to apprehend; may God grant us the grace to survive each other!

Author Bio

Catherine Gruben Smith lives in the middle of Texas, which she begrudgingly admits is probably better than a magical tower. She grew up mostly in a dusty town in the southern New Mexican desert and will always carry the quirks. (Yes, New Mexico is a part of the United States, and no, she was not a missionary, and yes, you can drink the water.) It is her delight and privilege to be a housewife, mother, and an Earl Gray connoisseur. Another of her constant activities is trying to keep her dogs from terrorizing the house and neighborhood with their determination to be always underfoot and hungry. (The work of a dog lover is never done.) She has always been fascinated by the written word, philosophical reasoning, and good stories of bravery and honor. When not writing, reading, chasing children or dogs, Catherine can be found board-gaming, baking, hiking, or possibly broad sword fighting with her older brother. If you want a fuller explanation of Catherine, go and read Psalm 30. The heart and purpose of her life can be found there, especially in the last two verses.

catherinegrubensmith.com
catherinegrubensmith@gmail.com
posttenebrasluxbooks.com

Books by Catherine Gruben Smith

Dreaded King Saga:
A Son Rises
Reign Falls
Knight Duty
Heir Raising
Splitting Heirs

Knight Jobs Series:
Wail of the Wyrm

Parabaloni Series:
The Parabaloni
The Slingshot Effect
As the Eagle Flies
Solitaire
Adele Angst
Blind Leader
Gathering Shadows
Black Out

Faerytales of Deweot:
How to Unmake a Dragon
Faery Wings and Pirate Things

Sojourners:
Ravens Ruins
Ravens Rescue
Ravens Return
Ravens Refuge
Ravens Raid
Ravens Rebirth